CREDITS

A play, as produced, is rarely the work of one individual. During the rehearsal period, suggestions are accepted from everyone within shouting distance. Many of these suggestions are excellent, and all of them are used. It is impossible to list here the names of all the people responsible for "Strictly Dishonorable" as it stands; I thank them all, and spend my royalties to their good health. I will, however, mention one name and refrain from mentioning one other. The first, is that of Edward J. McNamara, creator of the rôle of Mulligan, whose contributions, "It just seems like never," and "Who do you think I am, Paul Revere?" are much the funniest lines in the play. The second is the name of the gentleman responsible for the "O. Henry" joke and the line about the "non-refillable ginger ale bottle"; he asked me to keep it quiet.

Strictly Dishonorable

A Comedy in Three Acts

by Preston Sturgis

A SAMUEL FRENCH ACTING EDITION

SAMUEL FRENCH

FOUNDED 1830

New York Hollywood London Toronto

SAMUELFRENCH.COM

STRICTLY DISHONORABLE
by Preston Sturges

was produced by Brock Pemberton at the
Avon Theatre in New York, on September
18, 1929, with the following cast:

(*In the order of their appearance*)

Giovanni, a Lookout.........JOHN ALTIERI
Mario, a Waiter............ MARIUS ROGATI
Tomaso Antiovi..........WILLIAM RICCIARDI
Judge Dempsey.............CARL ANTHONY
Henry Greene...........LOUIS JEAN HEYDT
Isabelle Parry...........MURIEL KIRKLAND
Count Di Ruvo.........TULLIO CARMINATI
Patrolman Mulligan...EDWARD J. MCNAMARA

Staged by Antoinette Perry and Brock Pemberton
Settings designed by Raymond Sovey
Clarence Taylor, Press Representative
J. N. Gilchrist, Stage Manager

CHARACTERS

GIOVANNI

MARIO

JUDGE DEMPSEY

TOMASO

ISABELLE PARRY

HENRY GREENE

COUNT DI RUVO

PATROLMAN MULLIGAN

CHRISTOFORO COLOMBO . . . . . Herself

CARUSO . . . . . Himself

A C T   O N E

The speakeasy of Tomaso Antiovi on West 49th St. 11:41

A C T   T W O

A rear apartment upstairs over the speakeasy. 12:40 A.

A C T   T H R E E

The same apartment upstairs over the speakeasy. 10:00

ACT ONE

↑↑↑

S C E N E

An Italian speakeasy in West 49th Street. About mid-night, a Saturday evening in Autumn.

Door R.2 leads into kitchen. Door U.R. leads into hall which runs from R. to L., connecting with the kitchen off R. and the street door off L. Arch U.L. leads into hallway stairs to apartments, upstairs can be seen through arch. Two windows in R. wall, but they are covered with heavy drapes and cannot be seen. Bar down R. Stool behind bar; stool in front of bar upstage end. Small door U.R. and Arch U.L. Mirror between two windows. Two tables before banquette. Chair R. of Table R. Chair below Table L. Wall telephone R. of banquette. Hall rack in hall. R. and between rack and stairs, small chair. Slot machine U.L. Portable phonograph on stool just above mirror. Radio R. of Arch. Table and 3 chairs L.C.

A T R I S E

MARIO, *a waiter, is reading tabloid newspaper at table U.L.C. The radio is playing.* GIOVANNI *is seated in hall listening to music.*

GIOVANNI
La musica é una gran bella cosa.
> MARIO *turns off radio angrily, then reads.* GIO-VANNI *enters, puzzled, then turns on radio. He goes back to seat*

MARIO
Come é possible sentire a questa robaccia.
> *Turns off radio.* GIOVANNI *rises and comes into room*

GIOVANNI
Che diavolo succede. Bada di non toccare niente.
> *Turns on radio and hides behind arch R. side.* MARIO *tears paper in rage, then turns off radio just as* GIOVANNI *looks in and catches him by wrist*

A lazzarone! Ti hó detto. Di non toccare.

MARIO
Questo maledetto radio mi fá venire inervi.

GIOVANNI
Ma io hó l'ostesso diritto di sentire il radio come tu d leggere il giornale
> TOM *enters R.2 and crosses between them*

TOM
Silenzio! What's a matter with you people? You mak

ィィ

all noise when it's near to close. E questa tavola qui
senza sparecchiare.

> GIOVANNI *goes into hall. The iron gate is heard to*
> *slam and he goes off L. to answer it.* MARIO *folds*
> *napkins and orders table, then sits upstage and*
> *pulls tabloid from pocket and begins to read*

GIOVANNI
Off L.
Good evening, Mister Judge.

> JUDGE *enters, starting to stairs as* TOM *stops him.*
> GIOVANNI *sits in hall*

TOM
Goes upstage toward arch
Oh, Mister Judge, could you come in one minute, please?

JUDGE
I'm pretty tired, Tom. I want to get upstairs to bed.

TOM
Only just one little minute.

JUDGE
Entering to R. of TOM
What is it?

TOM
I make you one drink, huh? Then you no feel tired.

JUDGE
No. I've had a devil of a siege in court today and I'm
tired and weak.

TOM
I make one little Old Fashioned.

He crosses JUDGE *and starts to bar;* JUDGE *follows to front of bar upstage end*

JUDGE

I know your Old Fashioneds; don't make more than one.

TOM

Behind bar

All right, Mister Judge — all right.

Starts to mix drink

Judge, I got today a bigga trouble. I gotta paper.

JUDGE

What sort of a paper?

TOM

I don't know, Mister Judge. A man leava dis paper —

Takes summons from pocket

Suh — suh — summons to appear before the presiding mag — magistrato. I don't understand. I no do nothing.

Hands JUDGE *summons*

JUDGE

Let me see it.

Reads summons

Why — this is for contempt of court!

TOM

Me?

JUDGE

Sure. Tomaso Antiovi.

TOM

Corpo di Bacco! Contempt of court? Why, I do nothing. What means contempt for court, Mister Judge?

ィィィィィィィィィィィィィィィィィィィィィィィィィィィィィィィィィィィィィィ

JUDGE

Contempt? Why, it means you have no respect for the court — that you — ah — spit on it.

TOM

I spit? Cristo Santo! Never could I do such a thing, Mister Judge. I spit on the court? I do not even spit on the floor. I have admiration for the court. I love the court and all the fine judges — like you, Mister Judge.

JUDGE

Yeah — I know. Well now, let me see — you were summoned to appear on Tuesday. Why didn't you go instead of being in contempt?

TOM

I have no contempt. Why must I go last Tuesday?

JUDGE

Because you were caught speeding on Sunday.

TOM

It say that?

JUDGE

Sure it does.

> WAITER *rises guiltily and starts to straighten table, moving around slowly to L. and downstage as scene progresses*

TOM

Me make too much money to go joy ride. I no use the car on Sunday, Mister Judge.

JUDGE

You didn't lend your car to anybody, did you?

TOM

Lend my —?

> *Looks at* MARIO *and crosses to him.* MARIO *comes part way to him from front of table and they meet at L.C.*

Mario — Mario! You took my automobile —

MARIO

Si l'hó preso, ma non é successo niente.

TOM

> *Turning to* JUDGE

Yes, Mister Judge, he took the automobile, but he say nothing happen.

JUDGE

Did any policeman give you a paper?

MARIO

No, Mister Judge — only one small very little ticket.

TOM

> *Mimicking him*

Only one very little ticket —

JUDGE

Were you speeding?

MARIO

No, Mister Judge, no. I went so slow — like a snails I went — a sick snails.

JUDGE

> *Returning to bar*

You must have been obstructing traffic. Well, I guess it'll be all right.

> *Gives* TOM *summons*

ノノノ

TOM
Returning to behind bar
You fix it up, Mister Judge?
MARIO picks up glasses and bottles from table

JUDGE
Yes, I'll fix it up.

TOM
Thank you, Mister Judge — I'm very sorry.

GIOVANNI
Appearing in arch, mimicking MARIO
I went slow — like a snails, Mister Judge. Animale!

MARIO
Tartaruge! Lumacha!

TOM
Piano! Ssh! Ssh!
*They stop abruptly. GIOVANNI returns to chair in
hall; MARIO exits U.R. The telephone rings*
This is a SPEAKeasy. You make it sound like a LOUD-
SPEAKER!
He answers phone
Allo. Yes. His Excellency no come in yet, Miss Lilli.
No. . . . No. . . . No. . . . I don't know. . . . Any time
now. . . . Yes, Miss Lilli. You call again . . . all right.
Goodbye.
*Hangs up and goes to table U.R.C. Takes pencil
and makes note of call*
Alla time — alla time — womens call up — Miss Lilli
— Mimi — Miss Katie — Susie — Tessy — alla time —
too much for a singer!

JUDGE
Is Di Ruvo singing tonight?

TOM
Coming down slightly
No — no sing tonight. Sing last night. Pagliacci. I go.
Ah, Dio mio! The whole Metropolitan. Everybody, he
weep like an onions when he sing —
Sings
Ri di Pagliacci.
At finish of a snatch of song
Ah, he is grand!

JUDGE
Where is he? I want to congratulate him.

TOM
He go on big party, but he should be home now.
Looks at watch
He stay out too late. No good.

JUDGE
Why shouldn't he stay out late if he wants to? He isn't
a child.

TOM
Ah, to me, il Signorino is always a child — a little child.
I remember in Sorrento when he first arrive — when the
stork bring him and his father, il Signor Conte, come
all smiles and tell us servants: Open the wine, my good
friends, and drink to the health of my son who just now,
this minute, I have the pleasure to meet.

ͳͳ

JUDGE
Yes, but he's grown up now.

TOM
Ah, grown up. To me who see him so — and so — and
so — well, now he is so. But still he is not grown up.
When I tell him instructions from his mother, La
Signora Contessa, you know what he do — he laugh
at me.

> *Bell rings.* GIOVANNI *rises and exits L. in hall.* TOM
> *looks at watch again, shakes his head sadly as he
> returns behind bar*

Ah, too late — too late!

JUDGE
Nonsense. nonsense!

TOM
No nonsense, Judge — no good.

JUDGE
He can take care of himself.

GIOVANNI
Appearing in arch and holding up small card
Customers, Signor Tomaso.

TOM
Who are they?

GIOVANNI
Man and a lady — no come before.

TOM
They got card?

GIOVANNI
Yeah.

TOM
All right.

> GIOVANNI *exits R. in hall.* JUDGE *starts to arch*

JUDGE
I guess I'd better disappear.

> HENRY *appears in arch and looks in room*

Oh.

> JUDGE *returns and sits below bar.* HENRY *not pleased with place starts to leave*

TOM
Come in, Mister — come in.

HENRY
> *Turns to go; meets* ISABELLE

Naw. I'll come back some other time.

> *Sound of Gate off L. and* ISABELLE *appears in arch and enters room slightly, looking around*

TOM
What's the matter? You no like?

ISABELLE
> *R. side of arch*

What a lovely place, Henry. And look at that quaint little bar. Can we sit down?

> TOM *exits R.2*

HENRY
No. This isn't the place I thought it was. This is dead. I guess I got the cards mixed.

↑↑

ISABELLE
Crossing to L. end of table U.L.C.
I — I like it here, Henry.

HENRY
I tell you the other place is the one we're looking for.
The whole gang from the office goes there. They'll be
there with their wives.

ISABELLE
Let's not bother. It took an hour to park the car this
time.
Goes to chair R. of table L.C.
Let's sit down for a minute, anyway.

HENRY
Coming down slightly
I tell you if you saw the other place ...

ISABELLE
I wouldn't even know the difference, Henry. I've never
been in a speakeasy before and I'm afraid if we leave
this one, you'll just carry me home.

HENRY
Comes L. of table L.C. and sits
Oh — all right. But we'd be better off if we were home.

ISABELLE
Sits R. of table L.C.
Aw, no, we wouldn't. You gotta have a little fun sometimes.
*She opens pocketbook, takes out mirror and looks
at herself. Powders nose. Leaves pocketbook open
with* HENRY's *list easily accessible.*

HENRY

What's the matter with home?

> TOM *enters R.2 with bottle of cherries, placing them on bar*

Don't you like it there?

ISABELLE

Of course I do, Henry.

HENRY

Well, don't — talk that way about it then.

> *To* TOM

Hey, there — how about some service?

TOM

> TOM *rings bell.* MARIO *enters U.R.*

In a moment.

MARIO

> *Crossing to table*

You like a drink?

HENRY

> *Mimicking*

Yes, I like a drink. What do you think I came here for?
Bring me a double Scotch! What do you want, Izzy — a
liqueur?

ISABELLE

Whatever you say, Henry. It's all the same to me.

HENRY

And a crême de mint!

WAITER

> *As he crosses to upper end of bar*

One double Scotch — and one benedictine.

✔✔

HENRY

I ... SAID ... CRÊME ... DEE ... MINT! Now get it straight!

MARIO

No got any. S'alla same, anyway.

TOM

Maybe I got!

TOM *exits R.2.* MARIO *starts to read tabloid*

HENRY

Well, make it snappy!

ISABELLE

Don't get angry, Henry. You never used to get cross so easily. Why ... when ... when I first knew you, you were always smiling and ... and sweet. What's the matter with you, getting cross all the time?

HENRY

You didn't think I was going to be as sappy all my life as when I first met you, did you?

ISABELLE

Well, I hoped so. You said you'd be always like that and I'd ... learn to love you 'cause you were going to be so good to me. You weren't just making believe, were you?

HENRY

Of course I wasn't. But when a fellow's courting a girl, naturally ... he puts his best foot forward ... and ... puts up with a whole lot of damned nonsense he ...he wouldn't stand for all his life. Now when I sell bonds —

ISABELLE
You . . . you're not going to be nice to me any more?

HENRY
Of course I am, Isabelle. But you've got to be more SERIOUS. LIFE is serious. You Southerners are all alike. You think the sun shines just to make a nice day for you to go picnicking. It doesn't! It shines to germinate the wheat kernels to make your bread. It shines so you can have vegetables — fresh squash, beans, spinach —

ISABELLE
I hate spinach!
> TOM *enters R.2*

HENRY
Well, you don't eat the right food. But you will!
> *To* TOM

Say, do I have to wait here all night?

TOM
Just a minute, Mister. I got other customer. Must serve him first.

HENRY
You seem to be taking a long time about it.

TOM
An Old Fashioned take a lot of stuff.

ISABELLE
We're not in any hurry, Henry.

HENRY
Who said we're not? I want to get home.

ᛋᛋᛋ

ISABELLE

Not just yet, please. You know ... New York thrills me so, I'm happy ... just to be in it.

HENRY

Yeah? Well, it doesn't thrill me.
Drums table and looks over at TOM
Hey!

TOM

In a moment, sir.

ISABELLE

Could we — could we have our drinks at the bar, Henry?

HENRY

The bar is for men; you'd better stay at the table.

ISABELLE

Oh, but I wanted to ...
Resignedly
Oh, all right.

JUDGE

To TOM
They must be married.

ISABELLE

Not yet.
To JUDGE
But this is part of my trousseau.

JUDGE

Take your time, young woman, take your time. S'like going to jail: S'easy to get in, but hard to get out. I know. I'll tell you how I know. . . .

✓✓✓

Rises and starts toward them. HENRY *scowls at him menacingly*

HENRY

Yeah?

JUDGE
Crosses to bar
Some other time, my dear, some other time.

TOM

Mario!

MARIO

Subito!
Picks up tray of drinks, crosses to table and serves them — then exits U.R. to kitchen

HENRY
In an ugly mood
Well, it's about time . . . and say! Tell your friend tl jailbird to keep away from this table.

JUDGE
Crossing to C
Jailbird! Are you referring to me?

TOM

Ssh! Ssh! Ssh!

JUDGE
In a voice like thunder
Answer my question!

ISABELLE
Looks up at him and makes a pleading little gesture with her hands
Please. . . .

⬩⬩

JUDGE

At your service, Madam.

Turns to TOM

You know, Tom, I seem to be the only sober person in this place —

Turns to ISABELLE *and bows*

And you, Madam — and you. And this is no place for a sober man.

Starts to door U.R.

I'm going into the kitchen —

Turns at door

— where the eggs aren't boiled so hard.

He exits. TOM *exits R.2*

ISABELLE

Rising

I suppose we'd better get out of here, Henry.

She starts getting her things together

HENRY

Sullenly

There's no hurry. That old . . . Turk isn't going to drive me away!

ISABELLE

No, Henry . . .

Coaxingly

. . . but let's go anyway . . . and not have any more rows this evening.

HENRY *pounds table.* TOM *enters R.2*

HENRY

Bring me another Scotch.

TOM
S'pretty late ... Well ... one more maybe ... all right.

HENRY
Don't do me any favors.

TOM
Framed in doorway
Don't worry, Mister, I won't.

ISABELLE
Really, Henry, I'd much rather go.
TOM *rings bell*

HENRY
Harshly
Well, I'd rather stay.
MARIO *enters U.R. and goes to upper end of bar*
I suppose I'm in the wrong again.
TOM *exits R.2*

ISABELLE
No, you aren't!

HENRY
I suppose I should have let that old booze-hound get away with that stuff. . . .

ISABELLE
Sitting R. of table L.C.
No, Henry. You were perfectly right ...
MARIO *starts across to serve drink*
I mean it ... but sometimes I ...

HENRY
But sometimes you what?

↑↑↑

ISABELLE

Desperately

I mean . . .

MARIO *serves a double Scotch*

Thank you very much. . . . Now let's be happy. Here's to you, Henry. Here's to us.

MARIO *exits U.R.*

HENRY

Doggedly

Sometimes you what?

ISABELLE

Huh? Oh, I don't remember.

Sweetly

Let's forget about it.

HENRY

Let's *not*. If you've got any private thoughts about me, I'd rather know them . . . BEFORE we're married. If I had any private thoughts or criticisms of you, I'd tell you about them.

ISABELLE

I'm sure you would, dear, you're so . . . frank.

HENRY

Well, you be frank, too!

ISABELLE

It's nothing really, except that I'm not used to all the ways up here.

HENRY

Well, the people are different.

ISABELLE

Oh, not really, I guess, but . . . down home everybody's
sort of friendly like . . . that's all.

HENRY

That's only because it's a little town. You'll find the
same thing once we're settled in West Orange. . . .

ISABELLE

I . . . I don't think we'll find it in West Orange, Henry.

HENRY

What's the matter with West Orange?

ISABELLE

Oh, nothing.

HENRY

Isn't everybody there friendly to you? The family's certainly been nice to you, hasn't it?

ISABELLE

Of course, Henry. Naturally everybody I've *met* has
been nice. That isn't what I'm talking about. It's the
whole *feeling* out there that isn't . . . cordial. Don't
you see?

HENRY

Frankly, I don't.

ISABELLE

No . . . I don't suppose you do. But . . . but . . . that's why
I don't want to live in New Jersey.

✓✓✓

HENRY
Facing her across table
You . . . you . . . don't . . . want . . . to . . . live . . . in . . .
New Jersey!

ISABELLE
No, Henry, I don't.

HENRY
But that's . . . ridiculous! I've never *lived* anywnere else.
I've never *considered* living anywhere else.

ISABELLE
I know, dear.

HENRY
All my family's lived there always. I was born there.
Why, it's *beautiful* in New Jersey.

ISABELLE
Yes, Henry . . . But I don't like it.

HENRY
I suppose you're going to tell me Yoakum, Mississippi, is
a better town than West Orange. That little dump!

ISABELLE
I never said I wanted to live in Yoakum all my life. . . .
I don't boast about it.

HENRY
You don't bo . . . Well, I should say you wouldn't. Good
Lord! You come from Yoakum to West Orange. . . . .

ISABELLE
From Hell to Heaven?

HENRY

Well, I wouldn't have said it. . . .

ISABELLE

Of course not, dear, you're too polite.
She smiles at him quizzically
Aw, listen to me, Henry. I'm not ungrateful. It was
sweet of your mother to ask me to visit you all and give
me those two pretty dresses. I think you're all just as
nice as you can be: sweet and thoughtful and . . . and
very elegant and . . . and . . . honorable and . . . and . . .
She makes a hopeless gesture
. . . but I don't want to live in New Jersey, Henry.

HENRY

Where *do* you want to live?

ISABELLE

Couldn't we have a tiny little apartment here? I've seen
pictures in "House and Garden" of such cunning ones
. . . with little kitchenettes and . . . and . . . built-in wash-
tubs and things. Couldn't we afford that, Henry?

HENRY

Of course I could afford it . . . but you couldn't run it.
You can't even take care of your own stuff, let alone
manage a whole apartment!

ISABELLE

I could manage it.

HENRY

No, you couldn't!
Takes list from her pocketbook

↗↗

How about this little list of things I asked you to do yesterday?

                    ISABELLE
I did 'em.

                    HENRY
Yeah?
      Reading from list
"Purchase six white broadcloth shirts for Henry. Size fifteen and 34 inch sleeve. . . ."

                    ISABELLE
I got 'em.

                    HENRY
Yeah . . . you got 'em! Thirty-five and a half inch sleeves so Mother had to sit up half the night shortening them . . . you can't even sew.

                    ISABELLE
I can embroider.

                    HENRY
That's practical! And another thing . . . did you go to the Insulex Office and get their booklet on heating an eight-room house all winter on a ton of coal?

                    ISABELLE
I don't think you can.

                    HENRY
Never mind what you think, did you?

                    ISABELLE
I . . . I forgot.

↑↑↑

HENRY

Check!
> *Checks off item*
Now did you go up and look at that lot?

ISABELLE

Uh-huh.

HENRY

Well?

ISABELLE

I don't like it.

HENRY

What are you talking about? Why, that's one of the finest lots in town. In the heart of a restricted neighborhood, near a playground ... for the kiddies, only a block from Mother's, a block and a half from the church ... what's the matter with it?

ISABELLE

It hasn't got any trees on it.

HENRY

Good! What are trees good for, anyway — except for a lot of damned birds to roost in and wake you up at four o'clock in the morning!

ISABELLE

Oh, Henry. . . .

HENRY

Besides, you'll be a lot better off near Mother, so she can show you how to manage things.

ↆↆ

ISABELLE

I want to live here, Henry.

HENRY

I've already told you I don't like New York ... rotten, dirty place. I want to be some place where I can exercise and take long walks, where I've got room to BREATHE.

ISABELLE

Don't you think you could do that here? Everybody looks as if they breathed all right.

HENRY

Yeah — carbon monoxide!

ISABELLE

I don't know anything about that, but I read in a paper where people out in the country die much sooner than people in a big city.

HENRY

That's not statistics!

ISABELLE

Well, it said so in the paper.
She looks away despondently
Aw, Henry, couldn't we live here for a while anyway?

HENRY

Disagreeably
Well, you can live where you like ... but *I'm* going to live in West Orange.

ISABELLE

After a pause
Then I will too, Henry. . . .
She smiles with an effort
. . . and . . . and maybe it'll be very nice.

HENRY

You bet it will!
Patronizingly
Well now, that's settled! You just leave your happiness
to me, and you won't have a thing to worry about.

ISABELLE

I . . . I know I won't, Henry.

HENRY

Pompously
That's the way to talk.
ISABELLE *rises and starts towards the bar*
Where are you going?

ISABELLE

Stopping C.
Just over here. I . . . I want to put my foot on the rail.

HENRY

I think you'd better stay at the table.

ISABELLE

Over her shoulder
Please, Henry. Let me do a little bit what I like — till
we get married.
*She goes to bar, putting foot on rail and laughing.
Her arm hits bell accidentally. She laughs and*

rings bell again, then pounds twice on bar. TOM
enters R.
HENRY *rises — goes up to Victrola and starts to
wind it*

TOM
Yessir?

ISABELLE
Pretending to be an old souse
Gimme a drink.

TOM
Smilingly
Yessir, what you want?

ISABELLE
What've you got?

TOM
Baccardi, Manhattan, Bronx, Silver Fizz, Golden Fizz
...Old Fashioned.

ISABELLE
Ooн! I think I'll go back to my boyhood days and have
an Old Fashioned.

TOM
Yessir.

ISABELLE
Will you join me, Henry?

HENRY
Crossing to Center
No, thanks — I've got a Scotch. You'd better stick to
Crême de Mint.

ISABELLE
But that just tastes like sugar-water. Henry, I'd like to
have something real while we're here.

HENRY
You want to get drunk, huh?

ISABELLE
Course I don't — it's only an Old Fashioned — and old-fashioned people never got drunk — leastways, that's what I always heard.

HENRY
By the way . . . who's paying for this?

ISABELLE
Looking in pocketbook
Oh, I forgot, I haven't any money, Mister.

TOM
Don't you worry, young lady — no pretty girl has to go thirsty in Tom's place.

ISABELLE
Toward HENRY
There, Henry. You see? That's what I call friendly. Thank you, Tom, very much.

TOM
'S all right, lady, Any time.

HENRY
Back to Victrola
Oh, I'll pay for it.

ISABELLE
No, Henry.
Back to bar
We couldn't allow that. Could we, Tom?

↑↑↑

TOM

Yes, mam.

He puts the completed drink before her

ISABELLE

You should say no.

TOM

Yes, mam.

ISABELLE

Well, anyway . . . Here's to you, Tom.

She drinks

That was *delicious*.

TOM

In a whisper

You want another one?

ISABELLE

Yes.

JUDGE

Enters U.R., going to bar

Say, Tom . . .

He sees ISABELLE

Make me one of those too.

ISABELLE

Is feeling slightly emancipated already

They're mostly fruit-juice, anyway.

TOM

Smiling wickedly

Mos'ly.

HENRY
Looks up and sees his enemy, the JUDGE, *behind the bar; he stiffens*
Haven't you been at the bar about long enough?

ISABELLE
No, Henry,—I'm having a lovely time.
She sits on stool, upper end of bar

JUDGE
Goes to table U.R.C.
Whyn't you get wise to yourself, Henry? I'm not trying to swipe your girl.

HENRY
Meets JUDGE *center*
You'd have a swell chance.

JUDGE
Comes C. slightly
Well ... well, I guess you're right. There is something about your manner that ... ah ... must be very fascinating ... to some people.

HENRY
You're very quick on the repartee, aren't you?

JUDGE
No ... not quick, Henry ... but sincere, Henry. Come on — let's bury the hatchet — come and have a drink.

ISABELLE
Come on, Henry.

ィィ

HENRY

Oh . . . all right.
They cross to bar
But we'll make this the last.
HENRY *goes to lower end of bar*

JUDGE

Nonsense. Who's tired? Make that three, Tom . . . on my
bill. What do you want to go home for? It's early.

HENRY

Well, it may be early for you, but it's pretty late out in
New Jersey.

JUDGE

Why? Do they have different time out there?

HENRY

Of course not. But we live pretty far away. And we
might be locked out.

JUDGE

To ISABELLE
Oh, do they lock you out, too?

ISABELLE

Head of bar
Why . . . I'm . . . living with him.

JUDGE

But you said you weren't married.

HENRY

We're not, but —

JUDGE

But you're living in the same house?

HENRY

Yes, but —

JUDGE

In horror
Slightly irregular —

HENRY

Not at all — not at all!

JUDGE

Now let's get this straight; you're living together in
New Jersey, aren't you?

HENRY

Yes, but...

JUDGE

Just a minute.... Under the same roof?

ISABELLE

Oh, yes.

JUDGE

Crosses L. slightly
Well? There y'are. S'all right. S'none o' my business.
Turns
Say! You must think I'm drunk. Ha, ha, ha.

HENRY

Coldly
You're quite right. However, since you *will* mix into
other people's affairs . . . Listen carefully: This young
lady is engaged to marry me. She is living with my
parents in West Orange, New Jersey. Is that clear?

✔✔✔

JUDGE
Bowing low to Isabelle
I beg your pardon ... a thousand times.

ISABELLE
That's all right.

JUDGE
Turns to HENRY
And whom are *you* living with?

HENRY
Somewhat startled
Why, I live with them too. Naturally.

JUDGE
What do you mean: Naturally? I don't live with my parents. Tom, here, doesn't live with his parents. The young lady don't live with her parents.
Down to HENRY
Why should YOU live with YOUR parents?

HENRY
Well, I do.

JUDGE
Very suspicious.
To himself
Very suspicious.

HENRY
Time we were home.

JUDGE
To HENRY
Say, Henry, how is everything out there? Huh? How're the crops?

HENRY

The what?

JUDGE
Sits on edge of table U.R.C.

The waving wheat fields — the waving onion fields, all the little radishes — and things like that. SAY! What do you want to live in a place like that for, anyway? S'terrible!

ISABELLE
Crossing to him

That's just what I was saying.

JUDGE

Whassa name?

ISABELLE

West Orange.

JUDGE

Wes' Orange. S'awful.
He mimics

Where d'ya live? I live in Wes' Orange. Where's that? Why, it's just beyond South Banana before y' get to Eas' Pineapple. Nothin' but fruit stands. All Greeks.

HENRY

Yeah? Well, it was good enough for the men who fought the Revolution.

JUDGE

Certainly it was good e   ' for 'em. Anybody'd start a revolution if he lived in Pineapple, New Jersey. I'd start one myself — throw fruit at everybody — that's what I'd do. Say, now I'm beginning to understand, he's

↗↗

S C E N E

An Italian speakeasy in West 49th Street. About mid-night, a Saturday evening in Autumn.

Door R.2 leads into kitchen. Door U.R. leads into hall which runs from R. to L., connecting with the kitchen off R. and the street door off L. Arch U.L. leads into hallway stairs to apartments, upstairs can be seen through arch. Two windows in R. wall, but they are covered with heavy drapes and cannot be seen. Bar down R. Stool behind bar; stool in front of bar upstage end. Small door U.R. and Arch U.L. Mirror between two windows. Two tables before banquette. Chair R. of Table R. Chair below Table L. Wall telephone R. of banquette. Hall rack in hall. R. and between rack and stairs, small chair. Slot machine U.L. Portable phonograph on stool just above mirror. Radio R. of Arch. Table and 3 chairs L.C.

✔✔✔

JUDGE
Yes, but he's grown up now.

TOM
Ah, grown up. To me who see him so — and so — and so — well, now he is so. But still he is not grown up. When I tell him instructions from his mother, La Signora Contessa, you know what he do — he laugh at me.

> *Bell rings.* GIOVANNI *rises and exits L. in hall.* TOM *looks at watch again, shakes his head sadly as he returns behind bar*

Ah, too late — too late!

JUDGE
Nonsense. nonsense!

TOM
No nonsense, Judge — no good.

JUDGE
He can take care of himself.

GIOVANNI
Appearing in arch and holding up small card
Customers, Signor Tomaso.

TOM
Who are they?

GIOVANNI
Man and a lady — no come before.

TOM
They got card?

ↀↀ

ISABELLE
Crossing to L. end of table U.L.C.
I — I like it here, Henry.

HENRY
I tell you the other place is the one we're looking for.
The whole gang from the office goes there. They'll be
there with their wives.

ISABELLE
Let's not bother. It took an hour to park the car this
time.
Goes to chair R. of table L.C.
Let's sit down for a minute, anyway.

HENRY
Coming down slightly
I tell you if you saw the other place ...

ISABELLE
I wouldn't even know the difference, Henry. I've never
been in a speakeasy before and I'm afraid if we leave
this one, you'll just carry me home.

HENRY
Comes L. of table L.C. and sits
Oh — all right. But we'd be better off if we were home.

ISABELLE
Sits R. of table L.C.
Aw, no, we wouldn't. You gotta have a little fun some-
times.

*She opens pocketbook, takes out mirror and looks
at herself. Powders nose. Leaves pocketbook open
with* HENRY's *list easily accessible.*

ﻭﻭ

JUDGE

At your service, Madam.

Turns to TOM

You know, Tom, I seem to be the only sober person in this place —

Turns to ISABELLE *and bows*

And you, Madam — and you. And this is no place for a sober man.

Starts to door U.R.

I'm going into the kitchen —

Turns at door

— where the eggs aren't boiled so hard.

He exits. TOM *exits R.2*

ISABELLE

Rising

I suppose we'd better get out of here, Henry.

She starts getting her things together

HENRY

Sullenly

There's no hurry. That old ... Turk isn't going to drive me away!

ISABELLE

No, Henry ...

Coaxingly

... but let's go anyway ... and not have any more rows this evening.

HENRY *pounds table.* TOM *enters R.2*

HENRY

Bring me another Scotch.

ˈ✓✓

ISABELLE

Desperately

I mean . . .

MARIO *serves a double Scotch*

Thank you very much. . . . Now let's be happy. Here's
to you, Henry. Here's to us.

MARIO *exits U.R.*

HENRY

Doggedly

Sometimes you what?

ISABELLE

Huh? Oh, I don't remember.

Sweetly

Let's forget about it.

HENRY

Let's *not*. If you've got any private thoughts about me,
I'd rather know them . . . BEFORE we're married. If I
had any private thoughts or criticisms of you, I'd tell
you about them.

ISABELLE

I'm sure you would, dear, you're so . . . frank.

HENRY

Well, you be frank, too!

ISABELLE

It's nothing really, except that I'm not used to all the
ways up here.

HENRY

Well, the people are different.

ISABELLE

Oh, not really, I guess, but ... down home everybody's sort of friendly like ... that's all.

HENRY

That's only because it's a little town. You'll find the same thing once we're settled in West Orange....

ISABELLE

I ... I don't think we'll find it in West Orange, Henry.

HENRY

What's the matter with West Orange?

ISABELLE

Oh, nothing.

HENRY

Isn't everybody there friendly to you? The family's certainly been nice to you, hasn't it?

ISABELLE

Of course, Henry. Naturally everybody I've *met* has been nice. That isn't what I'm talking about. It's the whole *feeling* out there that isn't ... cordial. Don't you see?

HENRY

Frankly, I don't.

ISABELLE

No ... I don't suppose you do. But ... but ... that's why I don't want to live in New Jersey.

↗↗↗

HENRY
Facing her across table
You ... you ... don't ... want ... to ... live ... in ...
New Jersey!

ISABELLE
No, Henry, I don't.

HENRY
But that's ... ridiculous! I've never *lived* anywnere else.
I've never *considered* living anywhere else.

ISABELLE
I know, dear.

HENRY
All my family's lived there always. I was born there.
Why, it's *beautiful* in New Jersey.

ISABELLE
Yes, Henry ... But I don't like it.

HENRY
I suppose you're going to tell me Yoakum, Mississippi, is
a better town than West Orange. That little dump!

ISABELLE
I never said I wanted to live in Yoakum all my life. ...
I don't boast about it.

HENRY
You don't bo ... Well, I should say you wouldn't. Good
Lord! You come from Yoakum to West Orange. ....

ISABELLE
From Hell to Heaven?

HENRY
Well, I wouldn't have said it. . . .

ISABELLE
Of course not, dear, you're too polite.
She smiles at him quizzically
Aw, listen to me, Henry. I'm not ungrateful. It was sweet of your mother to ask me to visit you all and give me those two pretty dresses. I think you're all just as nice as you can be: sweet and thoughtful and... and very elegant and . . . and . . . honorable and . . . and . . .
She makes a hopeless gesture
. . . but I don't want to live in New Jersey, Henry.

HENRY
Where *do* you want to live?

ISABELLE
Couldn't we have a tiny little apartment here? I've seen pictures in "House and Garden" of such cunning ones . . . with little kitchenettes and . . . and . . . built-in wash-tubs and things. Couldn't we afford that, Henry?

HENRY
Of course I could afford it . . . but you couldn't run it. You can't even take care of your own stuff, let alone manage a whole apartment!

ISABELLE
I could manage it.

HENRY
No, you couldn't!
Takes list from her pocketbook

HENRY

Check!
> *Checks off item*
Now did you go up and look at that lot?

ISABELLE

Uh-huh.

HENRY

Well?

ISABELLE

I don't like it.

HENRY

What are you talking about? Why, that's one of the
finest lots in town. In the heart of a restricted neighborhood, near a playground ... for the kiddies, only a block
from Mother's, a block and a half from the church ...
what's the matter with it?

ISABELLE

It hasn't got any trees on it.

HENRY

Good! What are trees good for, anyway — except for a
lot of damned birds to roost in and wake you up at
four o'clock in the morning!

ISABELLE

Oh, Henry. . . .

HENRY

Besides, you'll be a lot better off near Mother, so she can
show you how to manage things.

✓✓✓

ISABELLE
I want to live here, Henry.

HENRY
I've already told you I don't like New York ... rotten, dirty place. I want to be some place where I can exercise and take long walks, where I've got room to BREATHE.

ISABELLE
Don't you think you could do that here? Everybody looks as if they breathed all right.

HENRY
Yeah — carbon monoxide!

ISABELLE
I don't know anything about that, but I read in a paper where people out in the country die much sooner than people in a big city.

HENRY
That's not statistics!

ISABELLE
Well, it said so in the paper.
She looks away despondently
Aw, Henry, couldn't we live here for a while anyway?

HENRY
Disagreeably
Well, you can live where you like ... but *I'm* going to live in West Orange.

HENRY
You want to get drunk, huh?

ISABELLE
Course I don't — it's only an Old Fashioned — and old-fashioned people never got drunk — leastways, that's what I always heard.

HENRY
By the way ... who's paying for this?

ISABELLE
Looking in pocketbook
Oh, I forgot, I haven't any money, Mister.

TOM
Don't you worry, young lady — no pretty girl has to go thirsty in Tom's place.

ISABELLE
Toward HENRY
There, Henry. You see? That's what I call friendly. Thank you, Tom, very much.

TOM
'S all right, lady, Any time.

HENRY
Back to Victrola
Oh, I'll pay for it.

ISABELLE
No, Henry.
Back to bar
We couldn't allow that. Could we, Tom?

TOM

Yes, mam.
> *He puts the completed drink before her*

ISABELLE

You should say no.

TOM

Yes, mam.

ISABELLE

Well, anyway ... Here's to you, Tom.
> *She drinks*

That was *delicious*.

TOM

> *In a whisper*

You want another one?

ISABELLE

Yes.

JUDGE

> *Enters U.R., going to bar*

Say, Tom ...
> *He sees* ISABELLE

Make me one of those too.

ISABELLE

> *Is feeling slightly emancipated already*

They're mostly fruit-juice, anyway.

TOM

> *Smiling wickedly*

Mos'ly.

HENRY
Looks up and sees his enemy, the JUDGE, *behind
the bar; he stiffens*
Haven't you been at the bar about long enough?

ISABELLE
No, Henry,— I'm having a lovely time.
She sits on stool, upper end of bar

JUDGE
Goes to table U.R.C.
Whyn't you get wise to yourself, Henry? I'm not trying
to swipe your girl.

HENRY
Meets JUDGE *center*
You'd have a swell chance.

JUDGE
Comes C. slightly
Well . . . well, I guess you're right. There is something
about your manner that . . . ah . . . must be very fascinating . . . to some people.

HENRY
You're very quick on the repartee, aren't you?

JUDGE
No . . . not quick, Henry . . . but sincere, Henry. Come
on — let's bury the hatchet — come and have a drink.

ISABELLE
Come on, Henry.

✔✔✔

HENRY

Oh ... all right.

> *They cross to bar*

But we'll make this the last.

> HENRY *goes to lower end of bar*

JUDGE

Nonsense. Who's tired? Make that three, Tom ... on my bill. What do you want to go home for? It's early.

HENRY

Well, it may be early for you, but it's pretty late out in New Jersey.

JUDGE

Why? Do they have different time out there?

HENRY

Of course not. But we live pretty far away. And we might be locked out.

JUDGE

> *To* ISABELLE

Oh, do they lock you out, too?

ISABELLE

> *Head of bar*

Why ... I'm ... living with him.

JUDGE

But you said you weren't married.

HENRY

We're not, but —

JUDGE

But you're living in the same house?

(39)

HENRY

Yes, but —

JUDGE

In horror
Slightly irregular —

HENRY

Not at all — not at all!

JUDGE

Now let's get this straight; you're living together in
New Jersey, aren't you?

HENRY

Yes, but...

JUDGE

Just a minute.... Under the same roof?

ISABELLE

Oh, yes.

JUDGE

Crosses L. slightly
Well? There y'are. S'all right. S'none o' my business.
Turns
Say! You must think I'm drunk. Ha, ha, ha.

HENRY

Coldly
You're quite right. However, since you *will* mix into
other people's affairs ... Listen carefully: This young
lady is engaged to marry me. She is living with my
parents in West Orange, New Jersey. Is that clear?

✓✓

JUDGE
Bowing low to Isabelle
I beg your pardon ... a thousand times.

ISABELLE
That's all right.

JUDGE
Turns to HENRY
And whom are *you* living with?

HENRY
Somewhat startled
Why, I live with them too. Naturally.

JUDGE
What do you mean: Naturally? I don't live with my parents. Tom, here, doesn't live with his parents. The young lady don't live with her parents.
Down to HENRY
Why should YOU live with YOUR parents?

HENRY
Well, I do.

JUDGE
Very suspicious.
To himself
Very suspicious.

HENRY
Time we were home.

JUDGE
To HENRY
Say, Henry, how is everything out there? Huh? How're the crops?

HENRY

The what?

JUDGE

Sits on edge of table U.R.C.

The waving wheat fields — the waving onion fields, all the little radishes — and things like that. SAY! What do you want to live in a place like that for, anyway? S'terrible!

ISABELLE

Crossing to him

That's just what I was saying.

JUDGE

Whassa name?

ISABELLE

West Orange.

JUDGE

Wes' Orange. S'awful.

He mimics

Where d'ya live? I live in Wes' Orange. Where's that? Why, it's just beyond South Banana before y' get to Eas' Pineapple. Nothin' but fruit stands. All Greeks.

HENRY

Yeah? Well, it was good enough for the men who fought the Revolution.

JUDGE

Certainly it was good ⸱ ⸱ ⸱ for 'em. Anybody'd start a revolution if he lived in Pineapple, New Jersey. I'd start one myself — throw fruit at everybody — that's what I'd do. Say, now I'm beginning to understand, he's

꿪꿪꿪꿪꿪꿪꿪꿪꿪꿪꿪꿪꿪꿪꿪꿪꿪꿪꿪꿪꿪꿪꿪꿪꿪꿪꿪꿪꿪꿪꿪꿪

a revolutionist — dangerous character. You want to be
very careful of a man with whiskers.

ISABELLE
Laughing
But Henry hasn't got any whiskers.

JUDGE
Oh, yes, he has, he's fooling you. Shaved 'em off. Prob-
ably got a pocketful of bombs.
Picks up drink at bar
Well, here's to a merry life in West Orange — New
Jersey!
Bell off L. rings
JUDGE *goes below bar and sits*

HENRY
Starting to table L.C.
We'd better get started.

ISABELLE
Crosses L. back of table to mirror
Please, not yet, Henry. I'm having a beautiful time.

HENRY
You know the family will expect us to go to church in
the morning.

ISABELLE
Oh, yes — I'd forgotten . . . still, let's stay a little bit
longer.

HENRY
Well, make up your mind. A few moments ago you said
you wanted to leave.

(43)

ノノ

ISABELLE

That was when you were cross. But now I'd like to stay.
Sometimes you're very sweet, Henry.

GIOVANNI

Off L.

Buona sera, Signor Conte.

HENRY

That's more like it.
Goes up to slot machine

GUS

Buona sera.

AUGUSTINO CARAFFA, *Count of Ruvo, appears
in arch. The sound of the gate closing is heard*

Good evening.

MARIO *appears in arch, takes* GUS's *coat and
muffler,* ISABELLE *is at mirror and sees* GUS.
HENRY *starts to play slot machine at intervals
throughout scene. On* GUS's *entrance he looks over
shoulder at him.* TOM *crosses to center to welcome*
GUS

TOM

Oh! Eccellenza . . . COSI TARDI!
*He looks at his watch and holds out his arms in
a supplicating gesture*

E le raccomandazioni della Signora Contessa? Cosa posso
scrivere alla Signora Contessa. . . . BUGIE!

GUS

Crosses to TOM *at Center*
Placatingly

GUS
Oh — just a few lemonades.
> *He turns again to* TOMASO

Tomaso, did any letters come for me?

TOM
> *Crossly*

No, Eccellenza . . . but a call from Miss Lilli,— and some packages. . . . No BUY so much. Spenda too mucha money!
> TOM *exits U.R.*

GUS
> *To the* JUDGE

Maybe my old Tomaso will forgive me when he sees what I have in the packages.

JUDGE
Why? What did you get?

GUS
Some surprises for him.

TOM
> *Entering*

Here are the packages for you.
> *He carries two packages, placing them on table U.R.C.*

GUS
> *Crossing to L. of* TOMASO

Not for me, Tomaso, but for you.

TOM
> *Opens packages*

Come?

ↂↂↂ

GUS

Yes! For you, old brontolone.
> *Gives stick and hat to* MARIO, *who exits up steps with them*

TOM
> *Pointing to himself and smiling*

For me?

GUS

Yes. And never again let me hear you complain about your rheumatism.

TOM
> *Opens box with violet ray lamp. Puzzled, he picks it up*

Cos' é questo?

JUDGE

What's that?

GUS
> *Taking lamp from* TOMASO

You shine it so. . . .
> *He demonstrates on* TOMASO

. . . where it hurts . . . and then it doesn't hurt any more.
> ISABELLE *drifts to L. of table L.C.*

TOM
> *Beaming*

Oh . . . Grazie, Eccellenze, ma perche spenda so mucha money per me?

GUS

Never mind that . . . now look in the other box.
> *Toward* JUDGE *slightly*

Now watch him . . . he will be like a cat with a . . . cat-nips.

TOM
Opens box and discovers it is full of India Figs, a sort of cactus
Ah! SANTO DIO! . . . FICHI D'INDIA!
Displays them to JUDGE
You — you like to eat some with me?

JUDGE
What — a cactus? Never!

TOM
He licks his lips greedily
Good! I go eat 'em right away to your health, Eccellenza.
He exits U.R. GUS *goes to door, watching him*
ISABELLE *is R. of table L.C.*

GUS
Yes, but think of YOUR health, and don't eat them too much. Funny old man . . .
HENRY goes up to arch and gets change from GIOVANNI
but very nice. Now we are friends again.

JUDGE
Rising
Gus, I want you to meet a very old friend of mine. This charming little lady is Miss . . . ah . . . Miss . . . what's your name?
GUS *looks at* ISABELLE *and starts toward her slowly*

ISABELLE
Crosses down to front of table
Isabelle ... Isabelle Parry.

JUDGE
Of course, Miss Isabelle Parry. The flower of the South,
Gus. Miss Parry, the Count Di Ruvo.
> JUDGE *goes behind bar*

GUS
Facing ISABELLE
How do you do, Miss Parry.
> *He bows low*

ISABELLE
Looking intently as if trying to place him
How do you do?

GUS
Turning to JUDGE *and crossing to* C.
Judge, this is most unkind of you.
> HENRY *returns to slot machine*

JUDGE
HUH?

GUS
I mean, a true friend, as you pretend to be, would not
have kept anyone so charming and beautiful all for himself. It was very selfish of you not to give me this great
pleasure before.

JUDGE
I want you to meet her fortunate escort, Mr. — ah —
Henry.
> HENRY *drops down several steps*

JUDGE

Is that so! Well, the way these new dogs spring up over-
night! They don't give you time to brush up on the old
ones.

As he goes to bar and sits on stove
Anyway, I know my Pekinese.

Telephone rings

GUS

I think we should offer a toast to such an expert and to
our beautiful guest.

Telephone rings again
TOMASO *enters U.R.*

Tomaso must find some champagne to celebrate the
presence here of — someone so lovely. And some Italian
chocolates.

MARIO *enters U.R. and goes to phone*

TOM

As he exits U.R.
Subito, Eccellenza — I go downstairs.

MARIO

At phone
Allo — yes — One minute, please.

MARIO *crosses down to* GUS

GUS

Crosses to ISABELLE
Do you like some champagne, Miss Parry?

ISABELLE

I've never had any.

GUS

You've never had any!

ꜱꜱꜱ

MARIO

Eccellenza la Signorina Lilli al telephone.

GUS

Angrily
Pantomime as GUS *goes to telephone and* MARIO
exits U.R.
At telephone
Hello — Hello — Who?— Oh, hello, Lilli — Not just now — I am in conference — No, don't come — I explain to you tomorrow — All right. I call you back in half an hour — good-bye.

Hangs up. ISABELLE *rises and crosses to L.C.*

ISABELLE

But, Mister Count —

GUS

Down to her
Di Ruvo.

ISABELLE

I know I've seen you before — it was recently. I'm sure we've met — I wonder where it was.

GUS

No, Miss Parry. I'm sorry to say we have not met. I wish we had.

ISABELLE

Thank you. But I know I've seen you —

JUDGE

Chair foot of bar
I guess it was in the Lucky Strike advertisement.

✓✓✓✓✓✓✓✓✓✓✓✓✓✓✓✓✓✓✓✓✓✓✓✓✓✓✓✓✓✓✓╲✓✓✓✓✓✓✓✓✓✓

ISABELLE

The Lucky —? Of course — that was it.

GUS

Such is fame.

HENRY appears in arch from R.

But we've never met. If we had — how could I have forgotten?

*TOMASO enters U.R. ISABELLE goes L. above table
L.C. TOMASO goes to table U.R.C. and places
champagne there*

TOM

Here is the champagne.

ISABELLE

*Seeing HENRY in mirror as he comes down to chair
L. of table L.C.*

Henry, you've seen those Lucky Strike advertisements.

HENRY

I don't like that guy!

He sits L. of table L. C.

GUS

*Toward ISABELLE as far as center with box of
chocolates*

Will you have some Italian chocolates, Miss Parry?

ISABELLE

Thank you.

TOM

There! One bottle of happiness! It turns your tears into laughter — makes you forget all your troubles. The sunshine of Italy in a bottle of Chinzano.

ISABELLE
Closing her eyes
What a heavenly voice. There's nobody else like him.

JUDGE
So you have heard him?

ISABELLE
Oh, yes, I've been to the Metropolitan three times to hear him sing.

GUS
Did you like him?

ISABELLE
He was marvelous. It was such a thrill! Of course I couldn't see him very well from where I sat...
She points to the ceiling
... but they say...

GUS
Perhaps it is just as well you couldn't see him ... so you can keep your illusions. Most of the singers are a little ... débordant. Only the birds can sing ... and keep their shape.
They all listen in silence till the record ends

TOM
Stands lost in the music and then comes to with a start and shuts off the machine. Then he turns and speaks to GUS with pride
Ah, my little Signorino, how you sing! I could listen to you all night.
To ISABELLE
He's some singer, huh?

TOM
The policeman outside wants to see you.
> *Goes to arch*

JUDGE
> *Steps forward slightly*
Perhaps if I . . .

HENRY
> *Rising*
I can manage all right, thank you.
> *To* TOM
How much do I owe you?

TOM
> *Back above table*
Two Scotch — one-fifty, one benedictine fifty cents — altogether two dollars.
> *Returns L. side of arch*

HENRY
You mean to say you charge seventy-five cents for that lousy Scotch?

JUDGE
That's all right, Tom — this is my party.

HENRY
Here you are.
> *Hands* TOM *a bill*
Leave the change on the table.
> *Goes into hall and gets hat*
> TOM *puts change on table*

HENRY
Come on, Isabelle.

ISABELLE

Below table

Oh, please, let's stay a little longer, Henry. I'm having such a nice time. See if you can fix it up with the—

JUDGE

Crossing to U.L.C.

If you'll allow me to say a word to the policeman . . .

HENRY

Returning U.L.C.

I don't need ANY HELP . . . from you.

JUDGE

But I think if I spoke to —

HENRY

There's nothing you could do, I couldn't do.

JUDGE

This isn't West Orange, you know.

HENRY

Picking up his change

I'll say it isn't. Come on, Isabelle!

ISABELLE

Coaxingly

Oh, Henry, please! Just a little . . .

Then seeing that he is adamant, she shrugs and begins slowly to gather her things.
The bell rings violently three times. Someone bangs the gate

TOM

You better hurry, Mister. I think Mulligan is getting mad.

HENRY

To hell with that guy!

ISABELLE

You'd better go, Henry!

HENRY

Looks furiously at ISABELLE *who is still taking her time*

All right. . . . But I'm coming right back. And then we're going home. Do you understand?

He stalks out — followed by TOM. *There is an embarrassed silence after he goes*

ISABELLE

Looks at the two men pleadingly. She is ashamed

He isn't . . . always that way.

GUS

Crosses to front of table L.C.
Consolingly

Of course not, my dear. We understand.

JUDGE

Returns, top end of bar

A charming fellow . . . at heart.

ISABELLE

Oh, yes, he really is, but —

TOM *enters in arch, coming R.C.*

TOM

They're having a lovely argument. The car is sitting in front of a . . . water faucet.

He exits at once to L. in hall

ɁɁ

ISABELLE
Goes up to arch
Perhaps we could help.

JUDGE
He said he didn't need any help. He's so sure of himself.
Aw, he'll get out of it all right.

ISABELLE
Returning to table L.C. for cape and bag
Goodbye! It's been mighty nice to meet you both. I
never met anybody famous before — I thought it would
be different —

GUS
But why?

ISABELLE
Oh, I don't know. I thought a famous person would be
very grand . . . and . . . and . . . but you're just . . .
like the people I like.

GUS
I am very glad you like such people . . . because I . . .
like you . . . very much.

ISABELLE
Thank you.

GUS
Crossing to phonograph
Do you think we could dance once before you go? Or
would Mr. Henry object?

JUDGE
Oh, Henry would be delighted.

(63)

ISABELLE

Backs up to table U.L.C.
Well, Henry's outside . . . he isn't here . . . and I'd like to dance with you.

GUS

Will you then?

She nods. He starts phonograph. They meet and dance

JUDGE

As he exits U.R.
Playing with dynamite — playing with dynamite.

GUS

You are very lovely!

ISABELLE

You shouldn't say that.

GUS

Why not?

ISABELLE

Because it isn't true.

GUS

But aren't you beautiful?

ISABELLE

No.

GUS

Very well.

He laughs
I . . . I love to dance with you, because you are very ugly. Is that better?

44

ISABELLE

I'm not so terribly ugly.

GUS

In feigned astonishment
Aren't you?

ISABELLE

No. . . . I'll get by.

GUS

Really!

ISABELLE

Oh, yes. But I'm not beautiful.

GUS

To me, Miss Parry, you are more beautiful than . . .
than . . .

ISABELLE

Than what?

GUS

Than I could ever imagine anyone to be.

ISABELLE

You shouldn't say that to me.

GUS

You are right. I shouldn't.

ISABELLE

And I ought not to like to hear it.

GUS

No.

GUS

Oh, yes — I know. I sing some plantation songs.

ISABELLE

They're pretty, aren't they?

GUS

Beautiful.

ISABELLE

I love to hear darkies sing 'em at night. Funny people!
Don't have anything...never did have anything...
never will have anything. And just as happy....You
ever been to Mississippi?

GUS

Where?

ISABELLE

Mississippi.

GUS

Mississippi?

ISABELLE

Yes.

GUS

Is that near Buffalo?

ISABELLE

You've never been there. We used to have a nice place.
And then, just when cotton got high, women stopped
wearing underwear.

GUS

Did women wear cotton underwear?

ィィィ.

ISABELLE
Silk underwear is immoral. That's what papa always said. He tried to get us all to wear cotton stockings, too, but we wouldn't do it.

GUS
I don't blame you.... Ah — were you a large family?

ISABELLE
No, just an ordinary family — four boys and seven girls.

GUS
Salute!

ISABELLE
Oh, that isn't big. Down home when they raise families, they raise FAMILIES.

GUS
And how!

ISABELLE
Well, they don't have much else to do.

GUS
And you are the most beautiful of the seven Parry sisters.

ISABELLE
Oh, no — they're all better looking — except one. One is uglier than me.

> HENRY *and* GIOVANNI'S *voices are heard in altercation off L.* ISABELLE *rises, goes to table U.R.C. and picks up bag*

But Mother is more beautiful than any of them.

> HENRY *rushes into room, followed by* TOM *and*

GIOVANNI. *Door in hall left open. He goes L.C.*
TOM *goes above table L.C.* GIOVANNI *remains in arch, leaning against it at Left. Gate is heard to slam.* JUDGE *enters R.2 and goes behind bar, sitting on stool and watching fight progress*

HENRY
Coming L.C.

Just what I thought! A grafting cop sees a New Jersey car parked near a hydrant, so he pushes it up in front of it, and then works a little blackmail.

JUDGE

How do you know he pushed it?

HENRY

Because I know he did!

To ISABELLE

And you want me to live in this rotten town! Come on, let's get out of here!

Goes to downstage side of table L.C. and picks up money, then goes upstage

TOM
L.C.

You like to stay and dance before you go?

HENRY
U.L.C.

No! Who wants to dance?

TOM

The young lady — she dances good.

HENRY
Downstage slightly

GUS

Crossing to her
But, not right away — I hope. We must talk these things over. I cannot lose you so soon.
Is now at bar

ISABELLE

Crossing L. to R. of table L.C. in front of GUS
He seemed so different from everybody down there that I thought he was different than they were. And I just this minute woke up. They were lazy and he was industrious. They liked to make love, gamble and likker up. Oh, they were bad all right and compared to them he was upright and honorable. But I guess honor isn't everything — do you think so, Judge?

JUDGE

Well, now, let me see. Speaking ex officio, I should say that honor ... or righteousness ... should be tempered with the milk of human kindness — that is if you can temper anything with milk. But I think too much honor is apt to curdle the milk.

TOM

Enters arch from L.
That fella come back. He wanta talk to you. I no let him in.
ISABELLE *moves up to* TOM *slightly*

ISABELLE

To the other two
Shall I talk to him?

GUS

Table U.L.C.
Do you want to?

ISABELLE

To TOM, with great finality
Tell him to go away.

> *Leans on chair R. of table L.C. She smiles triumphantly at her companions*
> TOM *exits L. in hallway*

JUDGE

Sits on stool behind bar, back to audience
Cruel woman.

ISABELLE

Tell me I was right, Gus.

GUS

I am afraid that I could not give an honest opinion. want so much for you to stay. . . .

ISABELLE

Looking at him sweetly
Oh!

GUS

Yes.

ISABELLE

That's nice of you to say so.

GUS

I would not say so if it were not true.

ISABELLE

Do you always tell the truth?

✔✔✔

GUS

Well — nearly always.

ISABELLE

I wonder.

TOM

Reappearing U.L. in arch

He's mad as Hell. I tell him to go away. He say No . . .
he stay. I say all right, Good night. He say: Listen, you
Wop, you, I break down the door. I say: I ain't no Wop,
go ahead and try. He say: All right, then, you Dago, I
go get an officer and make you all arrest for a-kidnap
the young lady. So I say I ain't no Dago, I'm Siciliano
and I poosh the door in his face. That's what I do!

He exits U.L.

ISABELLE

Running to bar

Do you suppose Henry will get an officer?

GUS

Going C.

Now, Judge, we're in your hands.

TOM

Appears in arch

He's out there with Mulligan the cop. Mulligan says
what's goin' on here. What'll I do, Judge?

JUDGE

Rises

Just a minute.

He thinks, then speaks to the other two

Gus, you take Isabelle in the dining room, and keep quiet.

> *They rise, and exit U.R. She takes all her things*

Now, Tom, bring Mulligan in here, but leave the young man outside. If he asks you why, tell him he isn't a member of this club.

> *Puts bottle of Scotch and two glasses on bar, then comes front of bar*

TOM

> *As he exits U.L. to door*

All right, Judge.

MULLIGAN

> *Appears in arch at C.* TOM *follows, standing L. of him*

Where is she?

TOM

Who?

MULLIGAN

The young lady.

TOM

No lady come to my speakeasy.

MULLIGAN

Don't use that word! How many times do I have to tell you I don't know what this place is?

TOM

I'll tell you.

MULLIGAN

Shut up! Now, where is she?

TOM

I don't know!

JUDGE
Turns
Officer! What are you doing in a speakeasy?

MULLIGAN
Crossing to C.
Well, bless my soul if it isn't my old friend Judge Dempsey. Shure, your honor, I'm here in pursuance of my duty.

> TOM *exits hall to Right.* JUDGE *starts toward* MULLIGAN

JUDGE
And what duty are you pursuing?

MULLIGAN
I'm pursuin' a kidnapper, your honor.

JUDGE
Meeting MULLIGAN *at C.*
Are you sure, now, that you're not pursuing an alcoholic beverage?

MULLIGAN
Shure, Judge, my tongue is hangin' out a foot, but I'm on the trail of a dangerous kidnapper.

JUDGE
A dangerous kidnapper, huh? My, what a wicked world. And who is this kidnapper?

MULLIGAN
Toward JUDGE, *slightly*
Ther're two of thim, your honor. One of thim is a

young Eyetalian, and the other one is an old, broken-
down barfly, a regular bum.

                    JUDGE
          Starting
Huh?

                    MULLIGAN
That's what the other fellow said. And they've stolen
a girl!

                    JUDGE
          Slightly vexed
Huh! Is that so? And where did you get this informa-
tion?

                    MULLIGAN
The young fellow who lost the girl is outside. Shall I
bring him in?

                    JUDGE
Don't bother. He's outside, huh? Well, well. And why
does he suspect that the damsel is secreted in this es-
tablishment?

                    MULLIGAN
          Puzzled
Yes — indade — to be sure.

                    JUDGE
I'm asking you: Why does he think the girl is here?

                    MULLIGAN
Oh! He says he lost her here. He was here earlier in
the evening.

✓✓

JUDGE
Puzzled
Oh, he was!

MULLIGAN
Yeah!

JUDGE
What does he look like? Was he a tall man, with a beard?

MULLIGAN
No, your honor, he's clean shaven.

JUDGE
With a broken nose?

MULLIGAN
No, not atall, he wears glasses.

JUDGE
Thinking hard
With glasses, huh? . . . Oh! THAT fellow — that Orange-man.

MULLIGAN
That what?

JUDGE
That Orangeman!

MULLIGAN
Stiffening
Oh, is he, now?

JUDGE
Oh, yes. He was talking about it all the time he was in here.

MULLIGAN
And I thought he was a dacent young fella.

JUDGE
You never can tell.

MULLIGAN
That's a fact.
He eyes the bottle surreptitiously

JUDGE
Crosses to bar, lower end
Would you like a little drink, Mulligan?

MULLIGAN
Shure, your honor, an' me tongue is like blottin' paper, but I never touch a drop whilst pursuin' a criminal.

JUDGE
And a very good rule too. How about a little ginger ale, out of a non-refillable bottle? That's what I'm having.

MULLIGAN
Crosses to top of bar — eyeing the bottle
Oh, ginger ale! With pleasure, your honor.
The JUDGE pours two stiff drinks
Well, here's to Prohibition, sor: a noble law.

JUDGE
Experiment.

MULLIGAN
Whatever it is.
They drink

ノノ

And what a wonderful improvement they've made in these soft drinks since the law went in.

JUDGE

That's progress for you.

MULLIGAN
He thinks a second, then scowls
An Orangeman, huh? And makin' all that trouble.
He pounds on the bar
They ALWAYS make trouble.

JUDGE
Tapping his forehead
I think he's crazy.

MULLIGAN

Naturally, your honor.

JUDGE

He was a terrible nuisance in here, always losing things.

MULLIGAN

Besides the girl, what else did he lose?

JUDGE

Well ... well, first, he lost a dog.

MULLIGAN

You're sure it wasn't a horse?

JUDGE

No, it was a dog! That's what he said, and we believed him.

MULLIGAN

Never believe an Orangeman.

JUDGE

Of course not. But we didn't know he was one then.

MULLIGAN

I'll bet there wasn't any dog.

JUDGE

That's what I suspect.
> JUDGE *goes* U.C.

MULLIGAN

Just a liar.

JUDGE
> *Starts to arch, slightly*

Yes, and when he came back from the street HE TOLD such a STORY, such a prePOSTEROUS, riDICULOUS, unbeLIEVABLE story, that we *knew* he was a liar.
> *Comes back to* MULLIGAN

MULLIGAN

What did he say?

JUDGE

HE SAID ... Well, he said, the OFFICER on this *beat* ...

MULLIGAN
> *Thinks this over. Suddenly he frowns*

HUH!

JUDGE

Yes, the officer on this beat had deliberately, and with malice aforethought, pushed his car —

MULLIGAN

Pushed his car—

✓✓

JUDGE

In front of a Municipal hydrant.

MULLIGAN

With malice aforethought —

JUDGE

And then — you won't believe your ears, Mulligan — had tried to extract from him a certain amount of United States currency, in other words, held him up for a bribe — not to arrest him.

MULLIGAN

Oh, he said that, did he? Well, he'll be lucky this night if he doesn't lose some of his teeth!

JUDGE

Of course, after that, we didn't believe anything he said.
Bell and pounding heard off L. Also HENRY'S *voice*

MULLIGAN

I think I hear a disturbance on the public highway.
Crosses JUDGE *as he starts toward arch*
Some drunk, no doubt. Perhaps a few hours in the cooler. Well, good night, sir, and many thanks for the ginger ale.

JUDGE

Center stage
Don't mention it. Oh — and Mulligan!

MULLIGAN

Stopping middle of arch
Yes, sir?

JUDGE

Observe the Law!

MULLIGAN

To the letter, your honor.
> *Starts off, stops*

JUDGE
> *Crossing to* MULLIGAN

You go ahead — but I'm coming right out to see that no murders are committed.

MULLIGAN

All right. But you could trust me to do the right thing.

JUDGE
> *L.C.*

That's just what I'm afraid of. And Mulligan!
> MULLIGAN *stops*

Don't use that stick!

MULLIGAN

Only in case of a tie.
> *He exits to L. in hallway*
> *Gate is heard closing*
> JUDGE *calls off R.*

JUDGE

Gus! Isabelle! It's all right. Come on back.
> *They enter*

ISABELLE
> *To R.C.*

What's happened?

GUS
> *To Center*

I am sorry to have made such complications.

ィィィ

ISABELLE

Are we to be arrested?

JUDGE

L.C.
I don't think so. In fact, I think by now Henry has probably changed his mind. Almost certainly has changed his mind.

ISABELLE

I guess he's cooled off.

JUDGE

I think Mulligan did say something about the cooler —
Goes up to arch

ISABELLE

The what?

JUDGE

Nothing — nothing. But I'll just go out and see that Mulligan doesn't get too excited.

ISABELLE

Up to table U.L.C.
I'm sorry to be such a nuisance.

JUDGE

As he exits to L. in hall
It's no nuisance — it's a pleasure.

GUS

Crossing to ISABELLE
Isabelle — may I call you Isabelle?
She turns and faces GUS

ISABELLE

Uh-huh.

GUS

Can you possibly forgive me? I'm terribly sorry for
you, but very happy for me. To think — you are alone
— with me. Do you know that you are adorable?

ISABELLE

Am I?

GUS

Very passionately
Yes.
*They stop dancing and he kisses her.
She fights a little, but not much*
I am mad about you.

ISABELLE

You're very convincing.

GUS

But, now, where are you going for tonight?

ISABELLE
Crosses down front of table L.C.
I . . . I don't know.

GUS

Follows her
You must . . . stay here.

ISABELLE

Huh?

GUS

With me.

ISABELLE
Looking into his eyes
What do you mean?

ⵎⵎⵎⵎⵎⵎⵎⵎⵎⵎⵎⵎⵎⵎⵎⵎⵎⵎⵎⵎⵎⵎⵎⵎⵎⵎⵎⵎⵎⵎⵎⵎⵎⵎⵎⵎ

GUS

Slightly ill at ease, looks away

I mean, I... I hope you will accept my hospitality —
until you find what you wish to do.

ISABELLE

For tonight?

GUS

For so long as you will honor me as my guest.

ISABELLE

Very slowly

But... have you room for me?

GUS

Certainly! In my living room is a divan so comfortable
... so embracing — so soft — it longs for somebody to
repose on it.

ISABELLE

Somebody like me?

GUS

Nobody else, Isabelle.

ISABELLE

But I don't want to be any more bother.

GUS

You — bother? Sweet child — will you be my guest?

Gate is heard off L. Then JUDGE *enters through
arch to center, speaking as he comes*

JUDGE

Well, Mulligan pointed things out to Henry very clearly.

Comes to C.

And now, young lady, to find a place for you.

ISABELLE

Well, he just said — he was kind enough to offer me — he said I could stay in the living room of his apartment for tonight.

JUDGE

But you're not going to?

ISABELLE

Yes — I am.

JUDGE
Glancing from one to the other
Well, in that case, I wish you a very good night then.
> *Goes up to arch on way to staircase.* ISABELLE *follows to front of table U.L.C.*

ISABELLE

Judge!
> *He stops and turns*

JUDGE

Yes?

ISABELLE
Hesitating
Good night.

JUDGE
Mumbling indistinctly
Good night.
> *He goes upstairs. She watches him a moment, then comes down to* GUS

ISABELLE

The Judge is afraid for me.

ↀↀↀ

GUS

Yes.

ISABELLE

What are your intentions toward me?

GUS

Smiling
Strictly dishonorable, Isabelle.

C U R T A I N

.

ACT TWO

✔✔

S C E N E

The living room of GUS's *apartment, upstairs over the speakeasy. It is a few minutes later.*

French windows and window seat R. wall. Covered canary cage hung upstage section of window. U.R.C. door leading to hallway of building. U.C., door to bath. U.L.C., door to bedroom. Grand piano and stool R. Keyboard set slightly upstage and to R. Music on same. Props to dress. Love Seat set in curve of piano, nearly parallel with footlight trough. Table just L. of this with Teddy Bear and picture of woman in frame. Down R., a small stand with drawers. Stockings in boxes in drawers. Book case R. of door U.R.C. Table between doors U.C. and U.L.C. On table, phonograph and telephone. Screen L. of door U.L.C. Small bed table below this and against L. Wall. Small bed lamp on same. Lamps on piano and on phonograph. Switch plate L. of door U.R.C. in wall. Large arm chair just L. of C. Divan, with cover, and fully made up with sheets and pillows, down R., head against L. wall. Foot of divan, small cushioned seat. Bathroom fixtures in bath, chest of drawers in bedroom.

A T   R I S E

*Stage is dark, except for moonlight coming through
French windows. Door U.R.C. is opened and* GUS *enters,
coming downstage slightly, turning and calling Up.*

GUS

Come in, Isabelle. Are you afraid?

ISABELLE

In doorway
Put on the light, please.

GUS

Switching on lights
Certainly. There.
He crosses to bed table and turns on light

ISABELLE

Entering to L.C.
So this is what it's like.

GUS

What what is like?

ISABELLE

A man's apartment.

GUS

Closes door U.R.C. and hooks chain
Yes . . . it is not so terrible . . . is it?

ISABELLE

No, it's lovely. Is this your own furniture — or do you
rent it?

ノノノノノノノノノノノノノノノノノノノノノノノノノノノノノノノノノノノノノノノ

GUS
Closes curtains on upstage window
No, it is mine. Tomaso — he is my landlord, you know — his taste in furniture is different.

ISABELLE
I suppose it is.

GUS
Comes around back piano to R. of chair L.C.
Yes. He likes... ah... massive mahogany... carved very elegantly with lions' heads and such things... and covered in green... how you say... ploosh?

ISABELLE
I know. We've got that kind down home... in the parlor. But ours was red plush.

GUS
In red it's more beautiful, no doubt.

ISABELLE
I think it's awful.

GUS
Do you? I am very glad then.
They laugh
Will you give me your things, please?

ISABELLE
She hands him cape and bag, which he places on upstage edge of piano. She crosses to Love Seat, kneeling one knee on L. end. She notes Teddy Bear
Oh, what a darling Teddy Bear.

✔✔✔

GUS
Turns R. of arm chair
It was given to me for Luck — and right away I meet you.

He drifts down C.

ISABELLE
Picking up hair pin below R. end of Love Seat
I didn't know women used hairpins any more.

GUS
Probably my cleaning woman dropped it.

ISABELLE
Probably.

Crosses to small stand D.R.
Is she blonde?

GUS
I ... ah ... never noticed. ... She wears a dust cap.

While ISABELLE *is examining ash tray, he sees photograph of woman on table L. of Love Seat. He turns it down quickly*

ISABELLE
Pushing cigarette end from tray
Well, you ought to tell her to stop smoking your cigarettes. It doesn't look nice to see the ashtrays all full of cigarette-butts with ... lip rouge on them.

GUS
Crosses to Love Seat. Kneels one knee on R. end
Darling — are you jealous?

ISABELLE
Me? No, just neat. You get that way when you've got

four big brothers tearing 'round the house and upsetting things.

GUS

Sits
You say your brothers are ... LARGE?

ISABELLE

R. of Love Seat
Oh ... not large. Why, the biggest one is only six feet two, and Charley, the baby, I don't think he's even quite six feet.

GUS

Practically ... a midget.

ISABELLE

No, but papa always said he'd be puny.

GUS

What a man. Your papa.

ISABELLE

Papa was a real man and when he died it took ten men to carry him.

GUS

I'm sorry.
Telephone rings. He smiles nervously, rises
Er — excuse me just a moment.
He goes to telephone. She goes to window and looks out
Allo. . . . Oh, yes, Lilli. I am still in conference. . . . We moved upstairs. . . . I don't know, probably very late. We are hardly beginning . . . no, I wouldn't come . . . it

would not amuse you. . . . Yes, dear . . . yes . . . yes . . .
yes . . . I do . . . I do . . . I do . . . very much . . . yes
. . . good night.

ISABELLE
Closing window
Your cousin again?

GUS
Down to L.C.
Oh, yes. . . . She . . . ah . . . she is one of those women
who wastes much time on the telephone . . . other people's time.

ISABELLE
Crossing in front of Love Seat
What is she like?

GUS
I don't know. She's really very charming. You must forgive my telling lies, but she wishes always to talk about
family matters. . . .
Crosses to ISABELLE
— and I do not like to talk about family matters . . .
tonight.
He embraces her

ISABELLE
Uh-huh.

GUS
Yes. How lovely you are . . . so young . . . so pliant . . .
so intoxicating. . . . So sweet — so gentle —

↑↑

ISABELLE

Breaking away slightly

I'm so pleased to hear you say nice things.

GUS

Darling, I'm so happy to have you alone with me — all
alone.

*She breaks away from him nervously to R. end
of Love Seat*

ISABELLE

Uh-huh, uh-huh, uh-huh —

*She is at downstage end of keyboard. She looks at
a piece of music*

Oh — this is your music?

GUS

Yes, darling.

ISABELLE

Will you — sing something for me?

GUS

Sitting on Love Seat

No, no, Isabelle.

ISABELLE

Why not?

GUS

Because, I am not Caraffa now. I am only me, Di Ruvo,
Gus, who — who is so happy to be alone — with you.

ISABELLE

But I —

GUS

No, no, no. Caraffa belongs to everybody. He is hang-
ing in his dressing room with his costumes. He waits for
his sweethearts — for Mimi, for Tosca, for Manon. He is
not lonely. It is Di Ruvo — Gus — who *was* lonely —
until he found his Isabelle.

ISABELLE
R. end of Love Seat
Is it like that to be famous?

GUS

Yes, it is like that to be alone, nearly always. To own a
talent like singing is like to own maybe a trained bear
that dances to make people laugh. The owner, he is
nobody, but the bear, he is everybody. The poor man
is invited to a party. What happen? So soon he arrives,
they say: Did you bring the bear? Or: Will you sing
for us a song? It is the bear, the talent, they want. For
him they care nothing.
*She crosses to his R. and stands there. He takes
her hand*

ISABELLE

I never thought of that.

GUS
Draws her to him slightly
No. Nobody thinks of it. But what do I care. Perhaps
you like a little Di Ruvo, huh? A little bit?
*There is a pounding coming from floor above.
They break in alarm, and she turns toward window*

ㅋㅋㅋㅋㅋㅋㅋㅋㅋㅋㅋㅋㅋㅋㅋㅋㅋㅋㅋㅋㅋㅋㅋㅋㅋㅋㅋㅋㅋㅋㅋㅋㅋ

ISABELLE

What's that?

GUS

It is the Judge — signaling to me from upstairs.
More pounding, then the JUDGE *calls down*

JUDGE

Gus. Gus.
GUS *rises and crosses to window*

GUS

As he crosses to window
Proprio al momento opportuna.
Calling out window
Hello.

JUDGE

Say, what's the date today?

GUS

The day?
ISABELLE *kneels L. end of Love Seat, listening*

JUDGE

The date.

GUS

Looking at watch
Sunday — since half an hour — already.

JUDGE

What?

GUS

Sunday.

Turns to ISABELLE
What is the matter with him?

JUDGE
No, no — not the day — the date.

GUS
To ISABELLE
What date is today?
Calls out window
The ninth.

JUDGE
Thanks.
He slams window

GUS
Crossing to foot of divan angrily. Back to R.C.
Seccatore, noioso.

ISABELLE
Watching GUS
I wonder what he wants so badly.

GUS
Oh, he probably suffers from curiosity.

ISABELLE
I like him. I wish he weren't angry with me.

GUS
Crossing to L.C.
I wish he would mind his own business. They are all
the same — these busybodies. Tomaso tells me how to
live; the Judge would tell me how to love. And neither
knows — they have already forgotten.
He crosses to her

Believe me, darling — believe me and you will know happiness.

Footsteps heard outside U.R.C.

ISABELLE

I wonder what that is? Do you suppose Henry —

GUS

Ssh.

Three raps on door U.R.C.

JUDGE

Off U.R.C.

Say, Gus —

GUS *takes chain off door.* ISABELLE *turns upstage and as* JUDGE *enters goes to R. of Love Seat.* GUS *goes L. of arm chair angrily*

May I come in?

Comes down to U.R.C.

Say, are you positive this is the ninth?

GUS

Absolutely.

JUDGE

S'my birthday. What do you know about that?

ISABELLE

Many happy returns of the day.

GUS

Congratulations.

JUDGE

Thank you —thank you both.

Crosses and sits in Love Seat

And now — now I'm going to save you both from a very dull evening. We're going to celebrate.

GUS

Here?

JUDGE

Now, don't apologize — this is good enough for me. I'm an old-fashioned man — don't like anything fancy. Tom will be right up with the champagne.

GUS

You — ah — told Tom to bring the champagne here?

JUDGE

Yeah, I telephoned down to him.
  GUS *laughs mirthlessly*

GUS

Oh.

JUDGE

This is my party. I'm taking care of everything.
  GUS *laughs again*
You — ah — didn't mind my giving a party here, did you, Gus?

GUS

Of course not, my dear Judge — I'm delighted.
  He laughs again and sits angrily in small seat foot of divan

ISABELLE

Me, too.

↗↗↗

JUDGE

Good. Let's have some music. You know, a party without music is like an egg without salt.

He goes up to phonograph, but before he can get it in readiness, TOM *enters with champagne and glasses*

TOM

Here is the champagne, Mister Judge. I am sorry it take so long, but that fellow come back.

Leaves door open and places tray on small table L. of Love Seat

ISABELLE

Downstage slightly in alarm

Who? Henry?

TOM

The policeman — Mulligan.

JUDGE

Down back of arm chair

What does he want?

TOM

He look for somebody.

GUS

Rising — up to L. of arm chair

Who is he looking for, Tomaso?

TOM

Looking for la Signorina.

GUS

La Signorina?

TOM

Yes. Il sus capolo hà mandato a cercare e dice che il signore di West Orange e qui, e va di la di qua, di su, di giu.

GUS

Calma. Calma, Tomaso. It would seem that Mr. Henry also told the sergeant that Isabelle has been kidnapped, so the officer —

JUDGE

Mulligan —

GUS

— has come back again with orders to search the house.

JUDGE

Oh, he has, has he? Tom!

ISABELLE
Returns to R. of Love Seat
What shall I do?

TOM

Hide in the Judge's room.

JUDGE

Alarmed
Not on your life!
Turns to TOM
Where is Mulligan?

TOM

When I come upstairs, he say he go look in the yard — behind the house in the back-house.
He points to window and crosses above piano to it

✓✓✓

JUDGE
Crossing to window below piano
I'll get rid of him all right.

Calling out window
Mulligan! Mulligan! Mulligan.

> GUS *follows* JUDGE *to window.* ISABELLE *is be-
> hind* GUS *to L.* MULLIGAN *enters U.R.C. and comes
> downstage several steps to left slightly. He watches
> them at window*

ISABELLE
Starting toward window
Do you suppose he'll find me?

GUS

Holding her back
No, darling, never! But don't show yourself at the
window.

ISABELLE
Could he come up here?

TOM
If he do, I kill him!

JUDGE
I'll have him broken!

GUS
He wouldn't dare.
> JUDGE *almost falls out window*

ISABELLE
Catch him, Gus.

GUS
Holding JUDGE *back*
I've got him.

TOM

Me, too.

JUDGE

It's all right. I see him. Do you see him, Tom?

TOM

Yes.

JUDGE

That thing that looks like a horse over there?

TOM

Yes — like a horse.

ISABELLE

Turns and sees MULLIGAN

Oh!

She recovers

Fancy seeing you here.

She nudges GUS

MULLIGAN

Fancy!

GUS

Turning

Oh.

He laughs nervously and nudges JUDGE, *who turns*

JUDGE

Oh — you!

MULLIGAN

Yes — the horse, himself.

TOM

Crossing to MULLIGAN

↗↗↗↗↗↗↗↗↗↗↗↗↗↗↗↗↗↗↗↗↗↗↗↗↗↗↗↗↗↗↗↗↗↗↗↗↗↗↗

I no mean to kill you, Mr. Mulligan.

> GUS *and* ISABELLE *are* R. *of Love Seat.* JUDGE
> *Crosses up to* R. *of* MULLIGAN.

JUDGE
What are you doing in here again?

MULLIGAN
The desk sergeant sent me back here to find her.

JUDGE
> *Crosses* L. *of* MULLIGAN

To find whom?

MULLIGAN
The young lady I was looking for.

JUDGE
It seems to me, Mr. Mulligan, you're always running after young ladies when you should be pounding your beat.

MULLIGAN

Judge!

JUDGE
Very suspicious. Very suspicious. I think you're lascivious.

MULLIGAN
Well — er — only on rainy days.

JUDGE
What about this young lady?

MULLIGAN
Your honor, it's just like I told you. I'm pursuing a dangerous —

JUDGE
Stop! Remember the straw that broke the camel's back
— remember the heel of Achilles!

MULLIGAN
I will! I've got fallen arches, myself. But I'm looking
for a young lady held against her will by villains!

JUDGE
Back of arm chair
Do you see any young lady being held against her will
by villains?

MULLIGAN
Not a sign of one, your honor.

JUDGE
You didn't think for a moment it was this young lady,
did you? Come here, my dear —
     ISABELLE *goes up between* MULLIGAN *and* JUDGE
— show the officer your wrists and ankles aren't tied.

MULLIGAN
Ah, the Judge is having his little joke.

ISABELLE
To GUS
Perhaps the officer would like some of your Italian
chocolates.

GUS
Front of Love Seat
I think he would much rather have a drink. Tomaso!
     TOMASO *starts to pour champagne*

ʻʻʻ

ISABELLE
But policemen never drink on duty!

MULLIGAN
It just seems like never.
> GUS *takes drink from table and returns to position*
> *before Love Seat.* ISABELLE *hands drink to* JUDGE
> *and one to* MULLIGAN

GUS
Here's to the police!

MULLIGAN
And here's to the people that send the police out on
false clues. Bless their little hearts!

JUDGE
> *To* MULLIGAN *significantly*

And here's to a long farewell.
> *They all drink and put glasses down*

MULLIGAN
Well, thanks very much for the ginger ale. And excuse
me coming in like this — it was orders.
> *Starts to leave;* JUDGE *stops him*

JUDGE
You'd better run around to all the other speakeasies
and see if you can find any kidnappers there.

MULLIGAN
All the other speakeasies? What do you take me for —
Paul Revere?
> *He exits U.R.C.* ISABELLE *comes R. of arm chair.*
> JUDGE *sits upstage end of foot of divan*

TOM

I go let him out.
Comes down to ISABELLE
Oh — la Signorina like tea or coffee?

ISABELLE

What?

GUS

Sitting Love Seat
Do you like tea or coffee?

ISABELLE
Nodding toward champagne
Why can't I have that?

GUS

For breakfast.

ISABELLE
Oh. . . . Oh . . . coffee . . . please.

TOM

Grapefruit?

ISABELLE

No, thank you.

TOM

And an egg.

ISABELLE

No, thank you.

TOM

Sausage?

GUS

Reprovingly
Tomaso.

✓✓

TOM

No hungry, huh? Tt. Tt. Too bad. You get sick. What time you want?

GUS

Finiscilla di parlare, Tomaso!

TOM

Va bene eccellenza. Good nigh', good nigh'. . . . Buona notte a tutti! Sleep good.

He exits U.R.C.

ISABELLE
Sitting R. arm of arm chair

He's nice. Have you known him long, Gus?

GUS

All my life. He was what you call . . . chamber valet . . . in my father's house.

ISABELLE

Chamber valet?

GUS

Yes. You know . . . he makes the beds and dusts . . . with a feather.

JUDGE

Housemaid?

GUS

The same work. But later he came to America. He's a rich man now. The food in his restaurant is famous.

JUDGE

That's why I never moved out of the house when he bought it and opened up his café.

ISABELLE

I see! It was very nice of you to come and live with him.

GUS

Well, my mother wanted me to. She's funny, my mother. Every month she writes a long letter to Tomaso, telling him what I should eat, and how it must be cooked and am I wearing my flannels and, I suppose, do I brush my teeth.

ISABELLE

How sweet of her.

GUS

Ah, well, to our mothers we are always little children, also when we get old.

JUDGE

Don't talk about being old on my birthday.

TOM

Knocking, then entering hurriedly

Eccellenza, eccellenza! Signor Conte!

GUS

Ma cosa c'è?

TOM

In a whisper

La signorina Lilli.

Describes her presence downstairs with pantomime

GUS

Starting to door U.R.C.

Ah, I must go downstairs . . . excuse me a moment.

JUDGE

Stops him

Has Henry —

ィィ

GUS

No, it is not Henry this time.

ISABELLE

Your cousin again?

GUS

Yes, Lilli —

ISABELLE

Why don't you ask her to come up?

GUS

Going to door U.R.C.

No. She is too old. You know — two flights of stairs is —
He exits. JUDGE *rises, crosses to table, fills glass
and crosses to Love Seat*

JUDGE

Now we can celebrate. Here's to you, my dear — look
well before the leap.
Sits on Love Seat

ISABELLE

Judge — I'm in love with him.
Crosses down to L. of and level with JUDGE

JUDGE

Isn't this rather sudden?

ISABELLE

I don't know. I've never been in love before.

JUDGE

But — but this other fellow?

ISABELLE

Henry?

JUDGE

Yes.

ISABELLE

I didn't love Henry.

JUDGE

Was that quite — fair?

ISABELLE

I told him I didn't love him.

JUDGE

Oh.

ISABELLE

He said I'd learn to love him — little by little.

JUDGE

Oh — an optimist.

ISABELLE

I think he read it in a book somewhere. I never heard of anybody learning to love little by little, like it was playing the piano or something. Did you?

JUDGE

I — ah — never studied the piano.

ISABELLE

I always thought it was *bang* — all at once, or not at all. And now, I know it's bang.

JUDGE

A big bang.

ISABELLE
Upstage slightly — looks at door U.R.C.
Uh-huh. So much so that nothing else matters very much.

JUDGE
How did you ever get engaged to Henry — although it's none of my business.

ISABELLE
Down to arm chair — sitting
Well, I had to get married some time; and my sisters all got the pick of the boys 'cause they were prettier —

JUDGE
Aw —

ISABELLE
Oh, yes, they were. So that only left Willie Borelle and Chet Lee when it came my turn to pick, and Willie's got the jitters —

JUDGE
Jitters?

ISABELLE
You know, he makes faces all the time — like this.
She distorts her face

JUDGE
Oh, my God.

ISABELLE
And both Chet's parents died in the State Asylum, and he said if I didn't marry him he'd shoot me, so I didn't marry him.

JUDGE

You were very brave.

ISABELLE

Well, he'd already told that to all my sisters, so I reckoned he was pretty safe. Besides, poppa always said: Never let anybody bluff you.

JUDGE

Your father was right.

ISABELLE

Uh-huh — he played poker that way. By the time he died our plantation was so small, we didn't know whether to try and grow cotton on it, or turn it into a croquet grounds.

JUDGE

And then along came Henry.

ISABELLE

Uh-huh — in a big shiny Buick. He was visiting over at the Sawyers'. Went to college with Buck. He liked me right away.

JUDGE

Can't blame him for that.

ISABELLE

Thank you. Had to carry me up to show me to his parents right off. They're all right — if you like that kind of people. Think they're better than my family. He was so sweet to me down home and then, soon's he got me North you'd 'a' thought I belonged to him.

✔✔

*She rises — goes up toward door and looks at it as
if waiting for* GUS *to return*
And I know now I couldn't belong to anybody — unless I loved him.

JUDGE
And you think you're in love with him?

ISABELLE
Turning downstage slightly
I don't think, Judge. When I heard that record and I saw him standing there like a bashful little boy, I said: Woman, prepare to see your dreams come true.

JUDGE
*Rises — looks at her a moment, then goes up to
phonograph table*
Young woman —
She turns up to him
Tonight you're going to a hotel — to the Martha Washington! And tomorrow you're going home!

ISABELLE
Backing toward R. a step or two
No, I'm not!

JUDGE
*Goes to piano and picks up her wrap and bag, then
putting them down again*
Do you hear me? Put on your things!

ISABELLE
Backs D.R. several more steps
I won't.

JUDGE
You will!

ISABELLE

I won't.

JUDGE

You're very unreasonable.
She smiles at him
I'll have you arrested.

ISABELLE

Front of Love Seat
You can't do that.

JUDGE

Oh, CAN'T I?

ISABELLE

No. You haven't got a warrant.

JUDGE

Ha-ha! I'll *show* you. . . .
He starts for secretary U.R.
. . . just give me a fountain pen and a piece of paper, and
I'll . . .

ISABELLE

You can't fool me. You're not a real JUDGE.

JUDGE

Down to above L. end of Love Seat
I'm not, hah? Well, by GOD. . . .

ISABELLE

It's just a . . . courtesy title.

JUDGE

Oh, it is, is it? Well, there are a lot of people in Sing
Sing right this minute who'd be glad to hear that . . .

↑↑

To Left, and return during laugh
... to wish I hadn't shown them so much courtesy.

ISABELLE
Sitting R. end of Love Seat
Judge!

JUDGE
Very suspicious
What is it?

ISABELLE
Even if you are a real judge, come and sit here . . . beside
me.

JUDGE
Starts to sit—checks himself
No, no! You can't weaken me with THAT STUFF. No
bribes. That's been tried before. They're all in jail!

Crosses to L.C.

ISABELLE
Sniffles
I think . . . I'm going to cry.

JUDGE
Going below chair to U.R.
Has no effect on me whatsoever!

ISABELLE *sobs*
Women's tears leave me cold.

Down to and above L. end of Love Seat
I hate women!

Goes U.R.C.
I like to see them cry. I enjoy it!

Down slightly to back of Love Seat
For God's sake, stop it!

ISABELLE

Still sobbing
Come here!

JUDGE

Going C.
I will not!
She sobs again as he starts R. He stops.
All right — stop it!
Crossing and sitting L. of her
Stop it, I say!
Pats her
There, there.
*She stops crying as he pats her, looks up at him
with a broad smile. He realizes she has deceived
him*

ISABELLE

I wonder where Gus is.

JUDGE

I don't want you to see him again!

ISABELLE

You can't send me home!

JUDGE

But I tell you —

ISABELLE

But, darling, you don't understand.

JUDGE

What! I don't understand WHAT!

ISABELLE

That I CAN'T go home. I went away to be MARRIED.

JUDGE
What of it?

ISABELLE
I can't go back like— *damaged goods*. YOU can't *do that* in a little town, no matter how innocent you are. They'd think there was something WRONG with me. Why, the whole of Yoakum would sit with its eyebrows up in the air for nine months just waiting and hoping for the worst.

JUDGE
They could wait as long as they liked— nothing would happen.

ISABELLE
Then they'd say nothing could happen.
> *She laughs*
I know my own home town.

JUDGE
Then what ARE you going to do?

ISABELLE
Gonna stay here . . . with Gus.

JUDGE
But . . .

ISABELLE
He SAID I could stay . . . as long as I liked.

JUDGE
Of course you know he won't marry you.

ISABELLE
> *Placidly*
I don't expect him to marry me.

JUDGE

He'll never marry!

ISABELLE

He's probably right.

JUDGE
Pounding cushion of Love Seat
I . . . won't . . . have . . . it!

ISABELLE

Now don't start again, darling. If I want to be foolish, let me be foolish . . . for once. I've always been sensible and good . . . you know it isn't much fun to be a girl . . . sometimes . . . and now I'd just like to drift with the current and not struggle any more . . . and for a little while . . . be happy.

JUDGE

I think you're immoral.

ISABELLE

Well, I read in a book of psycho-analysis that nothing is immoral except —

JUDGE

Except what?

ISABELLE

Oh, Lordy — I've plumb forgotten.

GUS
Entering U.R.C. and crossing to bedroom
Ah, forgive me — that Lilli — she makes me tired and hot. Women are so illogical —

ISABELLE

Oh!

GUS
At door U.R.C.
Except you, darling — except you.
He exits U.R.C.

JUDGE
Rises, goes to L. of arm chair and stops, turning to her and pointing his finger at her
And suppose you *do* have a baby!

ISABELLE
Very amiably
And SUPPOSE . . . I don't. They're not compulsory, you know.

JUDGE
What! Why . . .

ISABELLE
In the movies, darling. Only in the movies.

JUDGE
Where did you learn such things?

ISABELLE
Well . . . I've got five married sisters.

JUDGE
Starts to door, stops above chair
Well . . . REMEMBER . . . I WARNED YOU!

ISABELLE
Rises, backs D.R. slightly
Of what? You haven't warned me about anything.

JUDGE
Indignantly

✓✓✓

WHAT?

He comes back to center

Didn't I TELL YOU that you're taking the first downward step ... didn't I tell you that you're treading ... THE ROAD TO HELL?

ISABELLE

Why, NO. You didn't say anything about it ... you must have forgotten.

Crosses down to L. of divan. Crossing toward JUDGE *as far as L. end of chair*

Judge! You're a darling ...

JUDGE

Forgive me. I'm just an old busybody. I've no right to tell you how to find happiness ... When I never was able to find it for myself.

ISABELLE

Do you think I will be unhappy, Judge?

JUDGE

I don't know. You always hear of these things ending up ... in sorrow.

ISABELLE

Maybe you don't hear about them when they end happily.

JUDGE

Maybe.

ISABELLE

You see, I've never been very happy, Judge. I mean like I am now, because I never felt about anybody, like I do

about Gus. Don't you think, it's better to be very happy
for a little while . . . than never to be happy at all?

JUDGE
I don't know.

> *Goes above arm chair*

I don't know anything about it. All I know is you've
spoiled my birthday —

ISABELLE

> *Wheels to R. side of arm chair*

I'm sorry.

JUDGE

> *Meets* ISABELLE *at C.*

But I wish you'd give it a little more thought — will
you?

ISABELLE

> *R. of arm chair*

I will, Judge.

> *He goes to door U.R.C. She follows upstage
> slightly*

Good night.

> JUDGE *opens door*

JUDGE

Good night.

> *Starts out door and turns*

But if you do have a baby, I'll adopt it.

> JUDGE *exits U.R.C. She trails him to door, lingers,
> then comes down to upstage side of piano and
> picks up cape and bag. She looks toward bedroom
> door, then starts to door U.R.C. as* GUS *enters. She
> puts her things back quickly and starts to R.C.*
> GUS *is in pyjamas and lounging suit*

GUS
Coming L. of arm chair
Where's the Judge?

ISABELLE
Coming down R.C.
Gone to bed.

GUS
Good! What was he talking about so long?

ISABELLE
About C. downstage
Oh, happiness — and things like that. He — he wanted
me to go away from you.

GUS
And you?

ISABELLE
I didn't want to go.
Pause
But I think I'd better.

GUS
Down to her at C.
Darling!

ISABELLE
Warding him off
Don't you think I'd better?

GUS
Yes — I think you had.

ISABELLE
But I don't want to.

GUS
Come here!

ヽヽヽヽヽヽヽヽヽヽヽヽヽヽヽヽヽヽヽヽヽヽヽヽヽヽヽヽヽヽヽヽヽヽヽヽヽヽヽ

ISABELLE
If I stayed — would you promise not to say sweet things
to me?

GUS
Holding her hands
But, darling, I won't say sweet things to you if you don't
want me to.

ISABELLE
But I do want you to!
He starts to embrace her
Gus, couldn't you overpower me?

GUS
Backs away a step in surprise
What!

ISABELLE
Then it wouldn't be my fault.

GUS
Darling, you must not say such things.

ISABELLE
But I think 'em.

GUS
Listen to me, darling! A great man once said: "Thought
is the eternal rival of love." When you love, don't think
— just drift with the current of your heart.

ISABELLE
But that's just it. I'm a little frightened.
Starts to back R. slowly through next speech

GUS
Frightened? You? A great big girl like you? Who came

from Missis — well, where you said — here to New
Jersey to live with those cold storage family — and after
weeks with these ice boxes, you had the courage to face
Mister Henry. You are not frightened; I'll not let you
be frightened.

> ISABELLE *is downstage end of piano keyboard R.*

ISABELLE

Stop scolding me — stop it, I say. I won't let you scold
me.

> *Defensively, she picks up music from downstage*
> *end of piano. She looks at it*

Oh, it's in Italian. I always wanted to travel. Sing it
for me!

GUS

> *Crossing above piano to piano stool*

You're trying to be clever to avoid me.

ISABELLE

No, I'm not — honest! Please sing it for me.

GUS

Do you think you will understand?

> *She smiles*

Perhaps you will like Caraffa then — better than Di
Ruvo.

> *Takes music, sits at piano and sings. She is down*
> *extreme right, listening to him*

Donna Vorrei Morir!

Donna Vorrei Morir!

> GUS *rises and crosses down to her, taking her hands.*
> *He draws her over to a position below R. end of*
> *Love Seat*

ISABELLE

What does it mean, Gus?

GUS

Taking her in arms
It means I adore you!

ISABELLE

I wonder why that sounds so nice — even if it isn't true.

GUS

But it is true! Isabelle, kiss me!
They kiss and break

ISABELLE

Don't lie to me, Gus. The thing I like best about you is you've told the truth.

GUS

You are a strange little girl — I'm not sure I understand you.

ISABELLE

Up to R. of arm chair
I'm not sure I understand myself. I only know — that I'm happy to be here.

GUS

Thank you.

ISABELLE

Pointing to divan
Is that where the guest sleeps?

GUS

Crossing to lower side and head of divan
Yes, darling. It's more comfortable than my bed and it's all ready —

> *Pulls cover back, disclosing bed made up*
— see!
> *He crosses around foot of divan going to upstage end*

ISABELLE
> *Front of arm chair*

Pink sheets, ruffles and everything. Always made up ... in case of emergency!

GUS
> *Upstage end of divan, fixing sheets*

Sometimes a friend may want to stay ... if he misses a train.

ISABELLE

And have you pyjamas for the friends who miss trains?

GUS
> *Down foot of divan. Solemnly*

I think I can find a very nice pair of pyjamas ... that shrunk in the wash ... they should be just about right.

ISABELLE

And SLIPPERS?

GUS
> *Pensively*

I think it is just possible ... YES! when my sister was here she forgot a pair ...

ISABELLE
> *Merrily*

I THOUGHT you probably could find some. SOMEBODY must have forgotten some sometime.

ꜰꜰ

GUS

Looking at her feet
What adorable feet! ... You must wear about size three.

ISABELLE

Back R. several steps
Good heavens! Have you them in different SIZES? WHAT a man!

GUS

Crossing to embrace her
DARLING! You must not say such things ...

ISABELLE

I wouldn't have you any different.
He puts arms around her. She holds him off
Now, go and get the pygies and things.
He exits bedroom. She starts to untie belt of dress as she moves around from R. to L. side of arm chair. He enters with pyjamas and a pair of slippers. She puts belt of dress on L. arm of arm chair

GUS

Coming L. of ISABELLE
Here are the pygies and things. May I help you?

ISABELLE

Uh-huh.

GUS

Looking dress over
Where does it unbutton?

ISABELLE

You see where it unbuttons.

(139)

GUS

Shall I then?

ISABELLE

Uh-huh.

> *He starts to unhook dress. When she lifts dress over shoulders, she starts to speak*

I used to love to have my clothes taken off when I was too little to know how.

> *He takes dress and hangs it on screen U.L. She is now in Teddies, stockings and shoes. She sits on L. arm of arm chair, dropping stockings to below knees. He comes down, sits on seat foot of divan and takes shoes and stockings off*

I used to wear a lot more clothes when I was little... and Mama wore more than I did ... and Gramma wore more than all of us put together.

> *Stockings, garters and shoes are laid upstage end of small seat at foot of divan. He puts on slippers. As* GUS *puts slippers on*

Gramma said when she was a young girl, she wore three times as much as when I knew her —

GUS

Really.

> *Rises. She drops straps of Teddy over her shoulders. He takes top of pyjamas and puts it over her head. Teddy drops at her feet*

ISABELLE

I'll bet the men back in Gramma's day used to get awfully impatient waiting for the women to get undressed ...

˥˥

> *She picks Teddies up and places them on back of*
> *chair. Then she sits on arm of chair again*

to go swimming. But maybe they didn't swim much in those days —

> GUS *has pyjama pants. She slips her feet into them*
> *as he draws them up and over pyjama coat*

I used to wear things like that when I was a little girl only they had feet in 'em.

> *Pyjamas on, she rises, fixes her hair, then looks*
> *down at herself, slapping thighs of legs in protest*

No, no, no — the top goes on the outside.

GUS
> *Drawing top out of pyjama pants and laughing*

I must patent this.

> *He goes between foot of divan and small seat; she*
> *ties belt of pyjama coat. He holds his arm out to*
> *her*

Ah, Isabelle — my lovely Isabelle — come and sit beside me.

> *He sits foot of divan, she sits on small seat, re-*
> *clining in his arms*

GUS
Piccolo amore caro, tell me — what can you see in this ugly old opera singer?

ISABELLE
You're not ugly.

GUS
Do you like me a little?

ISABELLE
More than a little.

GUS

Why?

ISABELLE

I don't know — I don't think any woman knows. But it's like heaven to be near you — just your hand on my arm is like — I can't explain what it's like —

GUS

Don't explain. Words cannot explain such things. Words are only good for "How do you do?" — "Will you have some sugar in your tea?" Only for things that do not matter. No one must ever try to explain miracles with words. Darling!

Kisses her

I am mad about you.

Kisses her again. ISABELLE *rises, a little bewildered. She crosses to table L. of Love Seat. He follows her*

ISABELLE

I guess I — I'd like a little more champagne.

She hands him glass of champagne

Here's to you.

GUS

Here's to you!

They drink. Then put glasses down. He tries to take her in arms. She breaks away defensively

ISABELLE

Now — put out the lights.

GUS *goes up to switch. Lamps on piano and table between bath and bedroom doors go out. He starts*

*L. to bed lamp; she stops him. Going to front of
chair*
Except that one.

GUS
Starting to her
Angel!

ISABELLE
Meeting him L. of chair in embrace
Oh, Gus, I am happy!

GUS
It is I who am so happy.

ISABELLE
I love you.

GUS
But, darling, you are trembling. Are you then so afraid?

ISABELLE
I'm a little bit afraid.

GUS
But you must not be. Life is beautiful ... and its most
beautiful moments are called ... love. They are very rare,
my Isabelle, such moments as this ... to be accepted
tenderly ... and without fear.

ISABELLE
Don't ever let me go.

GUS
No, no — let you go? I'll hold you close — close to me.
My baby — like a child —
She breaks into sobs

↗↗

But you are crying.
>*They break*

But you are a baby!
>gus *backs upstage slightly as she crosses to L. end*
>*of Love Seat, her back to him and still sobbing*

ISABELLE
No, I'm not . . . don't girls usually cry?

GUS
Yes.

ISABELLE
Well . . . I'm no different from anybody else.
>*Then, out of a clear sky*

Do you think I'm pretty?

GUS
Hein?

ISABELLE
Do you think I'm pretty?

GUS
Of course I think you're pretty. You're lovely.

ISABELLE ·
Well, why don't you say so, then?
>*Turns to him angrily*

Isn't this the time to say sweet things to me? What are
you staying over there for? Don't you like me?

GUS
>*Rather emotionally*

It is because I like you so much . . . that I'm staying here.
You little . . . foolish!
>*Suddenly he makes up his mind*

↟↟

Now come here!
>*Crossing to her and taking her hand*

Come here, I say!
>*Leads her to divan*

Now get into bed!
>*She gets into bed and he stands over her upstage*
>*side*
>*Angrily*

Now listen to me: Never in my life before... have I done anything so stupid as now I am about to do... Do you understand? Never! Not once...I...I cover myself with ridicule... and I am... positive... that I will regret it forever. ALL MY LIFE. I will be angry for this moment. I...I... am CRAZY!

>*He strides over to table and picks up Teddy Bear.*
>*He returns to the bed and puts it down beside her*

THERE! So you won't be frightened.

ISABELLE
>*Clutching at the Teddy Bear*

I'm not frightened.

GUS
>*With an effort*

Now... GOOD NIGHT.

ISABELLE

What do you mean?

GUS

I mean...I will sleep tonight in the Judge's apartment. And You... YOU are going home tomorrow. Where your Mama can take care of you.

ISABELLE

I won't.
Then she sobs
Oh, Gus, you're horrid.

GUS

At the door
Yes, I knew you would thank me. Good night.
Goes up to door
Come here! Come here!

ISABELLE

She crosses to him, dragging Teddy Bear
What do you want?

GUS

Picking up chain on door
So soon as I have gone, you will place this end of the
chain in this receptacle . . . do you see?
He indicates it
. . . So if I change my mind, if I weaken, this chain will
be stronger . . . than my resolutions. Do you understand?

ISABELLE

Mulishly
I won't do it. I hate you.

GUS

You are a very bad girl. Good night.

ISABELLE

Aren't you even going to kiss me?

GUS

No.

ISABELLE

Aren't you going to put me to bed?

GUS

No!

ISABELLE

Then I'll scream!

She starts to scream. He picks her up and starts to
divan

GUS

Am I a nurse-maid that I have to take care so of babies?

Puts her on divan

Good night.

ISABELLE

Now kiss me!

GUS

Just a little one.

He leans over. She grabs him and kisses him
soundly. With difficulty, he breaks away

Now — hook the chain on the door, Baby!

He starts for door, U.R.C. She picks up Teddy
Bear and throws it on floor, crying as she does so

ISABELLE

I'm not a baby! I'm not a baby!

C U R T A I N

ACT THREE

ↀↀ

S C E N E

*Same as Act Two, except that the hangings on the center
section of French windows have been drawn. It is the
next morning and the sunlight can be seen stealing
through the curtains from off R.*

A T   R I S E

ISABELLE *is lying on divan, sleeping. There is a soft rap
on door and* TOM *enters, dressed in the uniform of a
valet de chambre. He carries a breakfast tray, which he
places on table L. of Love Seat. He picks up tray with
champagne and glasses and exits U.R.C. He returns at
once, crosses to French windows and pulls drapes open.
Then he takes cover off canary cage. The bird whistles.
He silences bird. He crosses to divan, picking up Teddy
Bear from floor and placing it at her side. He goes to
arm chair, takes chemise and places it over small seat
foot of divan. He looks at stockings on arm of chair and
finding a hole, he crosses to small stand D.R. Opens
drawer, takes out several boxes, looking at them until he
gets right size. Throws old stockings in drawer, crosses*

to chair and puts new ones on arm of chair. Goes to bed-room door, then down to bed, touching it to see if GUS *is there. She wiggles her feet. Returns to bedroom door, raps. No reply, looks puzzled. Raps on bathroom door. No reply. Opens it and looks in. Enters, turning on light. Looks at shower curtains to see if* GUS *is behind them, then turns on water. Enters leaving door open. Calls softly:*

TOM

Signorina — signorina — signorina.

> *She pulls cover over her head. He goes to phono-graph and plays record — "Stars and Stripes For-ever." She sits up angrily and throws Teddy Bear on floor. He picks it up and places it on piano, then closes phonograph*

Good morning, Signorina.

ISABELLE

Good morning.

TOM

> *To upstage head of divan*

I no see his Eccellency . . . any place.

ISABELLE

He's not here.

TOM

Not here?

ISABELLE

No.

TOM

That's very funny.

✓✓✓

ISABELLE

He's sleeping in the Judge's apartment.

TOM

Crossing to table L. of Love Seat

Well, chi va piano, va seno, e va lontano.

ISABELLE

Please don't play the piano.

TOM

No, I no play the piano. I go get your breakfast.

ISABELLE

I'd like a cup of coffee, if it isn't too much trouble.

TOM

No trouble —

Takes tea to her

I got for you a nice cup of tea.

ISABELLE

Are YOU going to boss me too?

He hands her a cup of plain tea

I'd like some cream and sugar, please.

TOM

No, no. No cream and sugar ... make you sick. Taka plain. Maka stomach swell up ... maka room for the eggs.

ISABELLE

I HATE eggs. I won't eat any eggs.

TOM

Very good for you. You eat eggs, and I give you sausage to poosh 'em down. THEN you feel fine.

Canary starts to sing

ISABELLE

Oh, Lawdy, couldn't you tell him to sing a little later?

TOM

You no like music?

ISABELLE

Not just now ... PLEASE.

TOM

I turn him off.

TOM *crosses to cage*

Silenzio! Ssh! Ssh!

Canary stops. A cat begins to meow. He hurries to table L. of Love Seat and fills saucer with milk

Ah, poosy, poosy, poosy.

ISABELLE

In despair

Bring him in. Bring him in. Let's have a party.

TOM

He's hungry.

ISABELLE

Well, for heaven's sake, give him those sausages. I hope he chokes on 'em.

↗↗

TOM

I give him a little cream. Here, poosy, poosy, poosy!
*Puts cream out window. Cat stops. Then he looks
at her a moment*
Ah, Cristoforo Columbo — what's the matter with you?
You getting fat again, huh?
As he crosses toward bathroom door
It won't be long, it won't be long.
Suddenly he rushes into bathroom
Every morning I forget.
Turns off water and re-enters
The bath tub ready, Signorina.

ISABELLE

I'll take a shower later.

TOM

Si, Signorina.

ISABELLE

You're not going to wash me, I hope!

TOM

No, no — no.
Takes tooth brush from drawer in table U.L.C.
I got for you a nice tooth brush.
Crosses to her with it

ISABELLE

It's not Lilli's, I hope.

TOM

Hands her tooth brush
No, it's a new one. You will find all different tooth paste

in the bathroom. Well, I go wake up Mr. Augustino
now, g'bye.

> *Takes her tea cup and crosses tray on table L.
> of Love Seat. Puts it on tray and goes to door.
> She stops him at door*

ISABELLE

Tom!

TOM

Yes, Signorina.

ISABELLE

Do — many young ladies come here?

TOM

No — just a few cousins and aunts.

> *He exits. She rises, crosses to C. Cat has begun to
> meow*

ISABELLE

Hello, Cristoforo Columbus.

> *Cat meows. She crosses to window and looks out*

You happy?

> *Cat meows*

You're going to have a lot of little pussies, huh?

> *Cat meows*

How many you going to have?

> *Three short meows*

You're going to have a whole family.

> *Turning to L.*

Gee, you're lucky.

> *Cat meows. Rap on door. She goes up R. of door*

Who is it?

JUDGE

Off U.R.C.

It's I!

ISABELLE

Come in.

*He enters and sees her in pyjamas. He is about to
leave at once*

Oh, I don't mind.

She goes to R. of piano

JUDGE

Well! And how is our little guest this morning?

ISABELLE

Listlessly

M'all right ... thank you.

JUDGE

At door

I was glad ... mighty glad ... to learn that you had
come to your senses last night ... but I always knew
you would. You can't fool me on CHARACTER ... that's
my business.

ISABELLE

I guess it would be hard ... to fool you.

JUDGE

IMPOSSIBLE! ... practically. And when Gus knocked on
my door and told me that you had sent him away ... I
wasn't a BIT surprised ... HE was, but *I* wasn't ... because I always KNEW you would.

ISABELLE
Did you?

JUDGE
Down to R. of arm chair
OH, yes! You know . . . there's something about a decent girl that . . . shows in the eyes.

ISABELLE
Moves to R. of Love Seat
Is there?

JUDGE
OH, MY, yes. To an expert, there is no mistaking the good . . . for the bad.

ISABELLE
I guess you know quite a lot about women.

JUDGE
Yes . . . ah . . . I do.
And he adds hastily
About GOOD women.

ISABELLE
Crosses to L. end of Love Seat
Judge, maybe good women are good because . . . because it takes two to be bad . . . and they can't find anybody . . .

JUDGE
Angry, up to door then to phonograph table
Rubbish!

ISABELLE
Well, of course you KNOW, Judge.

JUDGE

Yes, yes. Of course.
Starts down to her with ticket
I took a little walk down to Grand Central this morn-
ing, heh heh.
He laughs nervously and produces an envelope
... and while there, heh heh, I ... ah ... I bought you
this little present.
He hands it to her

ISABELLE

Hardly audible
Thank you, Judge ... I ... I ... thank you.
*She fumbles with the envelope and pulls out about
a yard of green ticket, starts to look at it*

JUDGE

I think you'll find it all there. There's quite a lot of it,
isn't there? Yoakum must be at some distance from here.
You know your home must be very beautiful this time
of the year. The fleecy clouds, the giant red woods, the
sparkling Pacific —

ISABELLE

Oh!
She drops down into Love Seat

JUDGE

Crosses to R. of her
Now, now, Isabelle ... be reasonable.

ISABELLE

Through her tears
How *can* I be reasonable ... I don't want to go to Ore-

gon when I live in Mississippi. You're just trying to get rid of me.

She throws ticket on Love Seat

JUDGE
Picking up the ticket and looking at it
Is it possible there can be TWO places with such a name. S'ridiculous!

ISABELLE
You don't have to insult me. Is it my fault, where I was born?

JUDGE
Now, now, Isabelle, I didn't mean that. The mistake is easily rectified.

He stuffs the tickets in his pocket
Now be a good girl and get dressed, and we'll go down there together, in a nice taxicab, and we'll fix it all up.

ISABELLE

Rises
Does ... Gus know that you're sending me home?

JUDGE
It was he who told me to get the tickets.

ISABELLE

Gus!

JUDGE
Yes. I forgot to mention it — it's a little present from both of us.

ISABELLE

Oh — oh, yes.

ノノノノノノノノノノノノノノノノノノノノノノノノノノノノノノノノノノ

JUDGE

Yes.

ISABELLE

After a pause

I ... I don't want to go home, Judge. I ... I can't go home. I told you so last night.

JUDGE

Up to her. Distressed

What ARE you going to do then?

ISABELLE

I don't know. I guess I'd better get dressed though.

JUDGE

Up to door U.R.C.

Yes ... Yes. And in the meanwhile I'll see if I can think of something. Don't be long.

He exits U.R.C.

ISABELLE

Walks into the bathroom. She re-enters and goes to phone slowly, not knowing whether to answer it

Hello ... Yes ... Yes, this is Mr. Caraffa's apartment ... Oh! ... Oh, hello ... Henry ... how did you find it? ... Oh, in the 'phone book ... that was right smart of you ... Yes ... Yes ... Yes ... you certainly were ... I think you'd better quit drinking ... all right ... all right ... I'll see you.

For the last word she drops her voice

... all right.

She hangs up very slowly

JUDGE

Off U.R.C.

Isabelle?

ISABELLE

Going to bathroom door

What is it?

JUDGE

Entering

Isabelle, I've been thinking and really the best thing you can do is to go home to your mother.

ISABELLE

You won't have to worry about me any more, Judge. I've made up my mind.

> *Goes into bathroom and* JUDGE *crosses to foot of divan. Rap on door U.R.C. It is* GUS

GUS

Isabelle! Isabelle!

> *Enters hurriedly U.R.C. Sees* JUDGE

Oh — you are here.

> *Looking around the room*

Where's the child?

> GUS *down to R. of arm chair*

JUDGE

She's dressing.

> *He indicates the bathroom*

GUS

Smiling happily at the bathroom door

I can't wait to see her. Oh, Judge! Congratulate me, felicitate me, shake me by the hand, kiss me on both cheeks, I'M IN LOVE!

JUDGE

HUH?

GUS

Ecstatically

Oh! It's WONDERFUL, it's MARVELOUS!

JUDGE

When did this happen?

GUS

This morning. About two o'clock. I couldn't sleep. I couldn't think. I got up, I listened to you snoring, STILL I couldn't sleep. I thought I was going crazy. I thought: Am I SICK? No. Am I HUNGRY? No. THIRSTY? No. Well, what DO I want?

He smiles languorously

And *then*, Judge, THEN I knew. OH, IT'S WONDERFUL to feel such a PAIN in the heart.

JUDGE

Sourly

It must be.

GUS

So THEN, what do I do? I take the telephone, I say give me Western Union, I say take a cable, please. And to my Mother I say: Mama Mia, I am in LOVE. With the most beautiful, adorable, enchanting, exquisite, lovely, pure, intelligent, remarkable, educated . . .

JUDGE

At fifty cents a word?

GUS

It was on your telephone.

JUDGE *sits on divan*

Faithful, obedient and irreplaceable maiden in the entire world and I humbly beg your permission to marry her. Answer immediately. Urgent. The answer should be here now . . . let me see: Two o'clock here is . . . seven o'clock in the morning in Italy . . . The cable would get there about nine . . . Mama would faint once with excitement . . . that takes about an hour . . . then she composes her answer . . . that takes another hour . . . then Giulio goes down to the telegraph office with the message . . . it isn't far, but he's old . . . that's another hour . . . then two hours for transmission, that makes nine o'clock . . . What time is it?

JUDGE

Looking at his watch
Eleven minutes past ten.

GUS

Crosses R.
Aie . . . Santo Deo. One hour and eleven minutes . . . late. They have *no* consideration. It would be quicker to send a *letter*. Or to go by street car —

Goes U.R.C.

JUDGE

Rises, crosses to C.
Now don't get excited, it'll be here. Hold your horses.

GUS

Crossing down to JUDGE
What do I want with horses? I want telegraphs.

JUDGE

There, there. Go and get dressed. It'll be here by the time you're ready. You're not going to propose in that, are you?

GUS

Hugs JUDGE

I'm a little bit excited . . . OH, IT'S MARVELOUS.

JUDGE

Suppose she refuses you?

GUS

My God, I never thought of that. I must look my best.

He starts up to bedroom, singing. Enters. JUDGE
goes up to R. of phonograph table. GUS *returns
with clothes. Shower increases in volume. He goes
to door U.R.C. Stops. Hears shower and comes
toward bathroom door slightly*

Oh! She's in my little bath tub.

JUDGE

Well, go and use mine.

Shower stops

GUS

Thank you.

Starts to go—stops

And, Judge — if she comes out — don't tell her anything — let me surprise her.

JUDGE

You can trust me.

GUS exits. JUDGE *comes D.C. then returns to bathroom door and raps*

ISABELLE

Offstage in bath
Don't come in.

JUDGE

Isabelle!

ISABELLE

What is it?

JUDGE

I've been thinking...

ISABELLE

So early?

JUDGE

I say I've been thinking...

ISABELLE

Just a minute.
She opens the door a little
What did you say?

JUDGE

I say I've been thinking...

ISABELLE

Drinking?

JUDGE

No! Thinking... with the brains... about you.

ISABELLE

Would you pass me that pink thing up there? What
have you been thinking with your brains about me?

˙ʎʎ

JUDGE
Well . . . after much thought, I've come to the conclusion
that perhaps you may be right.

ISABELLE
And now the stockings, please.
He gets stockings
Don't forget the garters!
Picks up garters, returns to door and hands them in
These aren't my stockings.

JUDGE
Well, it's a cinch they aren't mine!

ISABELLE
I guess they must be Lilli's. They're very nice though.

JUDGE
I have come to the conclusion . . .

ISABELLE
The what?

JUDGE
Shouting
The CONCLUSION . . . THE END.

ISABELLE
The end? Have you finished?

JUDGE
Paces back and forth front of door
No!

ISABELLE
Then why do you stop?

JUDGE
Tearing his hair
Oh, GOD!

ISABELLE
What?

JUDGE
Nothing. Now listen carefully . . .

ISABELLE
Will you pass me my dress?

JUDGE
Looks around room for dress
Dress? Dress?
Sees it on screen and takes it
Dress!
Takes it to bathroom
Here you are.

ISABELLE
Thanks. Now go right on — don't let me interrupt.

JUDGE
L. of door. Wearily
Well, as I was saying . . .

ISABELLE
Yes, go on.

JUDGE
I have been thinking, and . . .

ISABELLE
Just a second, darling, would you please —

✔✔

JUDGE

Anticipating her
All right— I'll get them.
*Gets slippers from upstage end of divan and hands
them in to her. Then starts to Love Seat, exhausted*

ISABELLE

Now, go on.

JUDGE

No, I'll wait until you're finished.
Sitting

ISABELLE

What did you say?

JUDGE

Wearily
I said . . .

ISABELLE

What?

JUDGE

God give me strength!

ISABELLE

*Enters dressed. Comes R. of chair. Stepping into
the room*
THERE! That didn't take long, did it?

JUDGE

Nooooooo! Not when you think of all the things I
handed you.

ISABELLE

You were sweet. Would you . . . would you hook me up?

JUDGE

Rising

Certainly.

> *Goes up behind her and hooks her up with difficulty*

There! You should have zippers on here.

> *Crosses to L. of chair*

ISABELLE

Thank you.

> *Goes R. and below chair*

Now what were you trying to say while I was in there?

JUDGE

What I was trying to convey, with remarkably little success, was, that after thinking matters over carefully, I've decided you were right.

ISABELLE

Of course I was right. What about?

JUDGE

About going home.

ISABELLE

You think I'd better not go?

JUDGE

To put it in a nutshell, yes.

ISABELLE

But if I don't go home, what WILL I do?

JUDGE

STAY HERE AND GET MARRIED.

✔✔

ISABELLE
Crosses to window
That's what *I* thought.
After a long pause
Even if I don't love him? ...

JUDGE
Great Guns! What's happened now?

ISABELLE
Maybe you're right. There doesn't seem much else to do.

JUDGE
He would be flattered if he heard you.

ISABELLE
I don't care ... I don't care about anything.

TOM
Knocking and coming right in
Signorina ... That young man ... who come with you last night ... he's downstairs ... insists he wants to see you. I no tell him you're here yet.

ISABELLE
L. end Love Seat. Sighs
Tell him to come up.

JUDGE
What!
Above chair

TOM
Exiting
Yes, Signorina.

ISABELLE
I don't think Gus would mind ...

JUDGE
What do you mean — he wouldn't mind — he'd be furious.

ISABELLE
Crossing to divan downstage side
No, he wouldn't.

JUDGE
Crossing to upstage side of divan
He would —
They start to straighten cover of chair
He would.

ISABELLE
I know.

JUDGE
Oh, I don't understand anything any more.

> ISABELLE *crosses to Love Seat.* JUDGE *puts two pillows on divan. He is about to get others when she turns and sees him as she sits*

ISABELLE
Never mind about that.
Rap on door
Come in.

> HENRY *enters.* JUDGE *brushes by him with a snort and exits.* HENRY *comes R. of arm chair*

HENRY
I . . . I came to apologize . . . Isabelle.

ISABELLE
That's all right, Henry.

HENRY
I said some rotten things. I'm sorry.

ノノノノノノノノノノノノノノノノノノノノノノノノノノノノノノノノノノノノノノ

ISABELLE

I said things, too.

HENRY

I was pretty drunk, I guess.

ISABELLE

I guess so.

HENRY
Eyeing the room surreptitiously
Did you . . . sleep . . . here?

ISABELLE

Yes, Henry. THERE!
She points to the divan

HENRY
From the chair
Nice apartment . . . in a flashy way.

ISABELLE

Do you think it's flashy?

HENRY
L. slightly
Yes — ostentatious.

ISABELLE
What's the matter with it?

HENRY

Ostentatious — Woppish.

ISABELLE
Well, I like it and the Count Di Ruvo said I could stay
as long as I liked.

HENRY
Viciously
Damn nice of him. And where would HE stay?

ISABELLE
I didn't ask him that.

HENRY
No . . . you wouldn't. But I can tell you where he'd stay, if you're anxious to know.

ISABELLE
I'm not.

HENRY
Where did he stay last night?

ISABELLE
Smiling slightly and looking at him
Where did YOU stay?

HENRY
Never mind where *I* stayed . . . where was HE?

ISABELLE
With the judge . . . your friend.

HENRY
How do I know he was?

ISABELLE
You don't . . . you never will.

HENRY
Toward her slightly
What do you mean?

ↆↆↆ

ISABELLE

Just that! If you don't believe me NOW, you never will, that's all. About THIS, or anything else.

HENRY

Narrowing his eyes

If I thought...

ISABELLE

You can think anything you like. I know how your mind works.

HENRY

Naturally I...

ISABELLE

I STILL have my virginity, if that's what's worrying you.

HENRY

Shocked

ISABELLE!

ISABELLE

Don't be a hypocrite... that's what you were thinking ... though why they make so much fuss about it is more than I can understand.

HENRY

Thunderstruck

FUSS ABOUT IT!

ISABELLE

You heard me. As if it mattered to anybody but me. By the way, I forgot to ask you! Are *you* pure?

HENRY

WHAT? Why...

ISABELLE
You needn't bother to answer. I'm not curious.

HENRY
It's ENTIRELY different anyway.

ISABELLE
Well, I don't REALLY know anything about it, so you may be right.

HENRY
Now you're being sensible. ·
 Smiles—several steps toward her
I ... ah ... hope you didn't take our little lovers' quarrel ... too seriously.
 ISABELLE *looks away, but says nothing*
We're ... still engaged, I mean.
 ISABELLE *remains silent. Edging closer*
Aren't we?

TOM
 Is heard pounding up the stairs yelling
Signor Conte, Signor Conte.
 He bursts into the room with a cable in his hand.
 He stands panting and looking around

ISABELLE
I guess he's in the Judge's apartment, Tom.

TOM
Thank you, I look.
 He rushes out
HENRY
 Watches him go, then
Isabelle!

ISABELLE

Yes?

HENRY

You didn't answer my question.

ISABELLE

Vaguely
Huh?

HENRY

Are you still my fiancée?

ISABELLE

Moving D.R. listlessly
I ... I suppose so.

HENRY

Follows to R. end of Love Seat
I knew you didn't mean it ... you couldn't.

ISABELLE *turns and looks at him without a trace of
a smile. Advancing*
Well, aren't you ... aren't you going to kiss me?

ISABELLE

Yes, Henry.

She is taken in his arms and kissed

GUS

Off U.R.C.
Isabelle!

Bursts into room with cable. Sees HENRY *kissing
her. She backs up against piano.* GUS *comes· to R.
of chair and stops*
I beg your pardon. The Judge said you wanted to see me.

HENRY
Up to R. of GUS. *All smiles*

It's quite all right, Count. It's OUR fault. By the way, Count, I want to thank you for turning over your rooms to my fiancée last night. It was very kind of you. I appreciate it.

GUS

I was only too happy.

HENRY

I also want to straighten out our little difference. I'm afraid I was intoxicated.

GUS
Stiffly

It is not necessary to mention it, sir.

HENRY

Well, then I guess . . . that's all.
Turns to ISABELLE
Are you ready, Isabelle?

ISABELLE

Yes, Henry.

> HENRY *goes to door U.R.C. and opens it. She picks up cape and bag, sadly; crosses L. toward* GUS *to L. end of Love Seat*

Good-bye, Gus.

GUS
Bowing
Good-bye, Miss Parry.

HENRY

Well, so long.

> ISABELLE *starts to go, and is stopped by* GUS's
> *words*

GUS

If you please . . . I would like to speak with you . . . for
one minute.

HENRY

Well, the fact is . . . we're in pretty much of a hurry . . .

ISABELLE

What is it, Gus?

HENRY

Coming to R. of GUS

Well, I suppose we CAN spare a couple of minutes.

GUS

To ISABELLE

Alone.

HENRY

Belligerently

SAY! What's the idea?

ISABELLE

Turning coldly to HENRY

This gentleman has shown me the greatest courtesy,
Henry. More than you can possibly realize. You have
nothing to fear in leaving me alone with him.

HENRY

I didn't mean that.

ISABELLE

Still in the same level tone

Will you wait for me in the car, please?

HENRY

Yeah, but —

ISABELLE

Are you going to start all over again, Henry?

HENRY

Going to door W.R.C.

Oh — all right.

Turns

But it's a damn funny idea.

He exits, leaving door open

ISABELLE

Looking at GUS *uneasily*

What is it, Gus?

GUS

Closing door. Very gravely

I came here just now . . . to ask you to marry me.

Goes down to R. and below chair

ISABELLE

Oh!

She turns to R., away from him

GUS

Yes.

ISABELLE

When did you get that idea?

GUS

This morning . . . after I left you. I couldn't sleep. I lay in bed wondering . . . wondering.

ISABELLE

What to do with me?

GUS

Yes.

ISABELLE

Then you thought of this ... solution.

GUS

Yes. Always you see, I thought marriage was not for me. For a woman, such life would be ... Hell. Here a few months, then quick to Milan, a week at La Scala, then two, maybe three days at home, then a rotten trip to Spain ...

> ISABELLE, *who has been only to Excelsior Springs, West Orange, N. J., and New York, listens to this itinerary breathlessly. She dreamily contemplates the wonders of such a trip*

... one week in Barcelona, one week in Madrid, then off to South America for the season. IT'S TERRIBLE!

ISABELLE

Yes ... it must be.

GUS

IT IS. IT'S AWFUL. So always I put behind me thoughts of marriage, so that some poor woman would not have to ... share my sufferings.

ISABELLE

That was very thoughtful of you.

GUS

But bad as it would be for the woman, think what it would mean for the children.

ISABELLE
Turns to him
Yes, I suppose it would be hard for the children.

GUS
Toward her slightly
TERRIBLE! But I will NOT be separated from my wife and children. I am, by nature, a family man. All my ancestors, on both sides, had families.

ISABELLE
Looking front, wistfully
I guess mine did too.

GUS
So can you see what it would be like . . . to travel? Nurses, valets, governesses, maids, toys, animals . . . Tutors, little boys, little girls . . . it would be like traveling with a menagerie!

ISABELLE
How many children did you expect to have?

GUS
I haven't decided yet.

ISABELLE
Oh!

GUS
But then this morning, I said, what the Hell, we only live once . . . if I can travel, the family can travel. So I put on my best suit, and came to tell you. And I find —
He extends his arm towards where she stood with
HENRY. ISABELLE *looks away from him*

✓✓

So now ... before you go ... out of my life into the arms of ... a younger man, I want you please to remember that I loved you, Isabelle.

ISABELLE
You don't.

GUS
Unheeding
... that I loved you. Very real ... very fine ... very honorable love. And when I lose you, I am losing something ...
He taps his heart
... of me. Something ... I am afraid I will not find any more.
In a more matter-of-fact tone
Something I did not deserve, Isabelle, because I have been a very wicked man. But that is no consolation for me now. You must go now.
He turns L. slightly
You must not keep Henry waiting ... the wife must be obedient and thoughtful.
Looks around at her
But if sometimes you hear me sing ... you will know I am singing for you, Isabelle, only for you, and ... and ... that is all.

ISABELLE
Up to R. of chair. Facing him
You don't love me.

GUS
> *L. of chair facing her*

Would I then have asked you to marry me? The only time in my life I ask anybody.

ISABELLE

And you were sure I'd say "Yes," weren't you?

GUS

No, Isabelle, but I hoped.

ISABELLE

Oh, yes, you were.

GUS

No, my child.

ISABELLE

You were sure I'd say yes because I couldn't do anything else. You felt sorry for me, and out of the kindness of your heart, you said, well, nobody else wants her, she's in trouble. I'LL take her. Well, I don't want your charity. I won't have it, yours or anybody else's.

GUS

But, I love you, baby —

ISABELLE

No, you don't.

GUS

But, Isabelle.

ISABELLE

You don't, you don't.
> *She is practically sobbing by now*

GUS

I do ... and you know it.

ISABELLE

You don't. YOU DON'T. If you did you wouldn't have left me ... last night, with that stuffed Teddy Bear.

She goes up to door and opens it

GUS

Putting up his hands

Baby!

ISABELLE

You're just trying to make me unhappy by telling me this now. That's what you're doing. Well ... it's too late. I DON'T love you ... I ... I love Henry. You saw me kissing him just now. You know what that means? It means ... that for the rest of my life ... I'm going to live ... in WEST ORANGE ... New Jersey!

She exits. JUDGE *appears in door, watching* ISA-BELLE *leave. Then he enters and comes down to R. of* GUS. GUS *passes cable to* JUDGE, *who looks at it a moment, then hands it back*

JUDGE

What does it say?

GUS

Below arm chair and L. Reading

Figlio mio: tu hoi il permesso e la mia beneizioned ...

JUDGE *interrupts*

Oh — excuse me —

Translates

My son — you have my permission and my blessing but ... there cannot be no such person ... you must be dreaming.

Looks up

✓✓✓

I guess she is right . . . my mother. I was dreaming.
> *The canary begins to sing. He crosses to front of*
> *Love Seat, back to audience. Throws cable down*

You can sing, Caruso, but I . . . I will never sing again.
> *Canary stops singing*

JUDGE

Oh, for God's sake, let's have a drink.
> *Phone starts to ring as he starts up to door U.R.C.*

I have something in my room.
> *He exits.* GUS *goes to telephone reluctantly*

GUS

Yes? Who? Oh, hello, Lilli, but the conference has just ended. No, it was not a success. I had hoped it would mean a long contract, but it was a complete failure . . . Yes, Lilli . . . No, Lilli, I cannot see you.
> JUDGE *enters, leading* ISABELLE. GUS *sees her and*
> *puts receiver on phone. Then he rushes down to*
> *her to R.C.*

JUDGE

Gus! Gus! Look what I found crying in my room! Isabelle!

ISABELLE

> *R.C. Down C.*

It wasn't true. I lied to you. I do love you.
> *Telephone starts ringing in jerks, then begins to*
> *ring regularly. They embrace and break*

GUS

But I warn you — I must have four sons and seven daughters —

✓✓

JUDGE
L. of door U.R.C. starting to exit
In that case I'll tell Henry not to wait.

C U R T A I N